AXLE

WAR BROTHERS MC

BIANCA LEE WARD

This book contains adult themes and is not suitable for persons under the age of 18.

For information regarding possible triggers, please see www.biancaleeward.com or contact info@biancaleeward.com.

Axle

<u>**Copyright**</u> © Bianca Lee Ward 2024

The moral rights of the author have been asserted.

All rights reserved.

Copyright Notice: No part of this book may be reproduced or transmitted in any form or by any means, electronic or mechanical, including photocopying and recording, or by any information storage and retrieval system, without permission in writing from the publisher.

This is a work of fiction. Names, places, characters, and incidents are the product of the author's imagination or are used fictitiously, and any resemblance to any actual persons, living or dead, organizations, events, or locales is entirely coincidental.

Warning: The unauthorized reproduction or distribution of this copyrighted work is illegal.

Cover Photo: Shutterstock 1097341256

Cover Designer: mariachristinepagtalunan@gmail.com

ALSO BY BIANCA LEE WARD

REAPER

War Brothers MC

I let her go once because she wasn't mine.

This time, I'll die before I give her up…

I want her.

That smile… those curves.

But Ava doesn't belong to me.

Then she arrives in my clubhouse, seeking refuge. My gut churns at the sight of the bruises on her face, the fear in her eyes.

Before I was the president of the War Brothers Motorcycle Club, I was a special forces sniper who hunted down evil men like her husband. Now I avoid relationships because the wounds I have are more than skin deep.

But Ava's different, and when I find her in the wrong bedroom—my bedroom—one night, what happens next changes everything.

I let her go once because she was married, but I won't make the same mistake twice.

I'll die before I let her dangerous husband, the jealous women in our club, or the enemy our club didn't see coming lay a finger on her.

Because this time around, Ava is mine.

Grab your copy of Reaper now.

BOMBER

War Brothers MC

I won't lose her again.

But our family secrets could tear us apart…

It's been ten years since I was forced to let Zara go. I joined the military and fought hard to forget her, but since I returned home to become our club's Sergeant at Arms, I've always watched from afar to make sure she's safe.

Now Zara is back in Crown Village on the anniversary of a traumatic event that changed her family forever. And I can't stay away.

I can see the longing for me in her eyes, yet she hesitates to get too close. She's scared to trust me again, and I don't blame her.

When new information linked to her family tragedy comes to light, I'm determined to help solve the mystery and find the answers she needs because the War Brothers MC protects our own.

But digging up the past means revealing secrets that someone wants to remain dead and buried. And when they're uncovered, they have the power to destroy our bond forever…

Grab your copy of Bomber now.

FRACTURED MIND

I'd forgotten my past.

But he hadn't forgotten me…

There was a life before the accident—a life that vanished when amnesia erased my first twelve years of memories.

With Mom burying her secrets in a bottle, I was left to piece together the fragments of my childhood on my own.

Now, back in the town where I was raised, I'm finally uncovering long-buried truths that shake the very foundations of my reconstructed memories.

I'm no longer the person I once was, and neither is my childhood best friend, Ashton De Santis. Ashton, now a fierce bare-knuckle fighter, protective and intense, slowly reintroduces me to our shared past. It's hard to ignore the spark of old feelings, but as our chemistry reignites, I can't shake the fear of getting burned.

Wanting Ashton is a risk I can't afford. Losing him a second time could haunt me forever.

Grab your copy of Fractured Mind now.

Sign up for my mailing list to be the first to hear all about book updates.

PLAYLIST

Just Like You – Falling In Reverse
Natural Disaster – Laidback Luke & Example
The Death of Peace of Mind – Bad Omens
I Knew You Were Trouble – Taylor Swift
Nowhere – Smooth feat. Tasha Baxter
Poison – Groove Coverage
Lead You On – Phix
Deadbeat – WesGhost
Underneath – Phix & Ryan Oakes
Sexy and I Know It – LMFAO
Up – Cardi B
Spine – WesGhost
Barley Breathing – Ashes to New feat. Against The Current
Curiosity – Bryce Savage
My Happy Ending – Avril Lavigne
Roses – Phix & Atlus
Wicked Game – Grace Carter
Hate Me – Ellie Goulding & Juice WRLD
Look What You Made Me Do – Our Last Night
Human – Elijah feat. Matty Mullins
Porcelain – Motionless in White
Until It's Gone – Linkin Park
Bad Things – I Prevail
Alone – I Prevail
Rollin' – Limp Bizkit
Even In The Dark – jxdn
I Think I'm Okay – MGK, YUNGBLUD & Travis Barker
Here With Me – Marshmello & CHVRCHES

ONE
A NEW HORIZON

Elena

"You have reached your destination," my phone's GPS app says. I pull over, mount the curb, and cringe at my terrible driving skills. I scan my surroundings and sigh in relief—no one saw that. It's late afternoon. Despite using a navigation app, I still got lost and could have arrived earlier.

The two-story redbrick house is average looking. It will be my new home in Crown Village, a small coastal town with a lake and beaches. I already know I'm going to love it here. My previous town just didn't feel like home.

Closing my eyes, I recall the first time I told my parents I was leaving.

Mom's mouth is wide; her eyes bulge and then narrow. "No! You're not leaving."

I clench my shaking hands in front of me. "I got a job as a waitress at a respectable restaurant." I smile, thinking if my parents see how happy it'll make me, they'll be happy.

"Why are you moving away from us?" Dad asks. "You

gave up college . . . now you're taking up *another* waitressing job away from us and your sister?" His disapproving glare slices through me like a blade.

I frown. I'll miss my sister, Ava, but that's about it. I shake my head to get rid of these thoughts—I need to stay positive.

Two girls in bikinis, with towels around their shoulders, rush out of the front door of the house and dash past across the lawn. They're probably going to the beach; it's not far. That's what the ad said, at least. I'm renting a bedroom in a shared house because that's all I can afford in this town. It's so expensive here.

When I step out of the car on shaky legs, the breeze swirls around me, flicking my hair. I inhale the fresh, salty air. I could get used to this. I had to escape my small hometown and experience life while I'm still young. A sudden flicker of nerves makes my heart pump in my chest. I roll my shoulders back. "Pull yourself together," I mumble under my breath.

After closing the car door, I walk across the lawn and stand by the front door. I knock. "Hello," I call out. It comes out as a strangled whisper, so I clear my throat to try again. "Hel—" is all I can say before the door opens right into my head. Pain ricochets through my forehead and nose.

"Sorry," the guy in the doorway says. He chuckles.

A girl opens the door fully. "Are you alright?" She's attractive and also wearing a bikini, and her blond hair is tied back in a super high ponytail.

"Yes," I say. I smile tightly, even though it still hurts. "I'm Elena. I'm supposed to be moving in today."

She gives me a big smile. "I'm Lucy. The owner told me about you. Your bedroom is the first one you see when you get up the stairs. I'll go get your keys." She darts away.

I swallow and look at my feet, conscious of the guy's eyes on me.

"Want to join us at the beach?" he asks.

When I look up, I try to focus on his face so that I don't stare at his body. He's wearing only shorts.

I peer back at my car. "I've got to get unpacked . . . but uh, thanks."

He nods. "Maybe next time," he says, and smiles.

Lucy comes back with an outstretched hand. "Here are your keys."

I take them from her.

"The small one is the key to your bedroom. Just lock it when you leave to go anywhere, because we have parties occasionally. The big key is to the front door."

"Thanks," I say hesitantly. Is she insinuating that there are thieves or that random people will barge into my room when they are over? I consciously make a note to lock the door 24/7.

"I'll see you later," she says, then I watch as the two walk away in the same direction as the other girls went.

I return to my car, open the back door, and retrieve my heavy suitcase. I tow it along on its wheels while I proceed to the house. The front door opens on the living room, which is furnished with weathered green couches. A few beer bottles are scattered on the tables. The house is basic, with white walls, worn floorboards, and the bare minimum of furniture. As I walk in further, I see the kitchen toward the back and a staircase to my left.

I drag my suitcase over to the stairs. I go up one stair, pull . . . two stairs, pull . . . My suitcase is so heavy. This is going to take a while.

I'm breathing heavily when I get to the top, but at least the door is only three steps away. I knock first, just in case Lucy directed me to the wrong room. Silence. I push the door wide and see a white metal bedframe with a mattress on top, a white chest of drawers, and a nightstand.

Two and a half hours had passed by the time I'd dragged

my suitcase and bags of clothes, shoes, books, and toiletries up the stairs and unpacked. I'm straightening the spines of my books when I hear laughter and talking coming from outside the house. The voices move inside and the front door bangs shut.

I step out of my room to hear a guy say, "I wonder if that girl is still here or if she bolted after seeing us." He laughs. "The look on her face and what she was wearing . . . it looked like she was going to church."

I glance down at my long dress with three-quarter sleeves and my ballet flats. What's wrong with my outfit? To be fair, I have worn this dress to church on Sundays many times, but still . . .

"Her name's Elena. I'm sure she's in her room," Lucy says. She looks up the stairs. Her friends follow her gaze until all eyes are on me.

I give them a small wave. I've always been socially awkward.

Lucy waves me over. "Come down and have some pizza with us."

My stomach growls, reminding me I haven't eaten since breakfast. I go down the stairs and approach her.

"Come on, I'll show you around," she says with a bright smile.

I clasp my hands in front of me and nod.

Lucy steps over to her friends, who have taken a seat on the couches. "Everyone, this is Elena," she says. She points to the three attractive girls. "These are my friends Cindy, Jasmine, and Lia. They all live here too." Cindy and Lia have blond hair, and Jasmine has black hair. The girls give me a friendly smile.

Two guys are fighting over the remote. Lucy points at one and says, "Jeremy is my boyfriend." It's the guy I saw this morning and who made fun of my dress. He snatches the remote and then smiles at me.

"Justin is Cindy's boyfriend," Lucy says, gesturing toward the other guy. He salutes me.

I follow Lucy toward the kitchen. The kitchen cabinets are cream, but with plenty of scratches. A broken cupboard door hangs crookedly. It's clear that no one is taking care of this house. I suppose it's perfect for people our age.

"Pots, pans, cutlery, and cups are stored in the cupboards and drawers," Lucy says. "The grocery store is only a short drive away. Write your name on things in the cupboard and stuff like milk so that no one gets confused about who it belongs to."

I follow Lucy back to the loud voices in the living room. Lucy sits on Jeremy's lap, and I take a seat on the single chair.

"Where are you from?" Lucy asks. Everyone quietens and all eyes lock on to me.

"I'm from Meadowbank. It's a small town around a thirty-minute drive from here." My hometown isn't anything to be embarrassed about. I need to be independent from my parents, and I thought a beach town would be a great place to move to.

"Oh yeah. It is small. It takes what, five minutes to travel through?" Lia asks sarcastically.

"Something like that," I answer.

"What brought you to Crown Village?" asks Jasmine as she twirls her long black hair around her finger.

I was lonely and bored. "I landed a job at a restaurant."

"Which one?" asks Lia.

"Crown Village Seafood Restaurant."

"Our friend Cameron works there. His parents own it. The food there is so good," says Justin. Everyone else nods.

"So good, but so expensive," says Cindy.

There's a knock on the door. Both guys stand up and hurry to the door. "Pizza's here!" Justin yells out.

"Where do you guys work?" I ask them.

Cindy's face contorts. "I don't work. I'm at college studying economics."

"I'm studying tourism," Jasmine adds in.

"Jeremy and I are studying business management," says Lucy. "Justin, engineering, and Lia, social sciences."

"So, you all study and don't work?" I clarify.

"Yep." Lucy nods, and I feel an inch tall. Their parents must pay for everything.

The boys walk in and place the cardboard boxes on the table. When they open them, a heavenly smell wafts out. Jeremy takes two large slices and sits back down before he crams as much as he can into his mouth. As I take a small slice of pizza and a napkin, I marvel at just how different I am from them. While they're out partying and sleeping in, I'll be working.

After my belly is full, I say good night and go to my room. I lock the door before I lie down.

I could have been like them. Going to college was an option for me. I got the grades for it. I considered majoring in English, but in the end I wasn't certain. I wasn't going to get into that much debt without being one hundred percent sure what career I wanted. I thought I was doing the smart thing. Taking time off to consider my options. But according to my parents, I have the brains, so I should be going to college and making something of myself, not just being a waitress on minimum wage.

My phone beeps. The message is from Henry, my ex-boyfriend, who I broke up with a while ago. We had been together since high school. He got into a college on the East Coast and intended to live on campus, but I didn't want to have a long-distance relationship. Besides, we had grown apart long before we broke up.

The breakup had been amicable, and we still talk occasionally. I'm glad that there's no bad blood between us and that we can still be friends. We've been close for so long.

Henry

How did the move go?

Good thanks.

At least someone cares, I think to myself.

I've met my roommates, they seem friendly.

That's awesome. I look forward to hearing about it all.

I go back to my home screen. No phone call from my parents, asking if I arrived safe or if I've settled in okay. They were less than pleased about me moving and said I'm making a mistake. I wanted—no, I needed—to get out from under my parents' judgement.

When I was searching for jobs, I saw a position as a waitress being advertised in Crown Village. Excited by the opportunity, I immediately applied. I was tired of being comatose, living but not alive. My roommates seem to be friends with the restaurant owner's son, so that's a positive considering they seem like a friendly group of people.

I pick up my reading glasses and put them on, then grab a romance novel from the nightstand and start to read. Soon I'm lost in stories about love, book boyfriends, and happily ever after, which are far better than my reality.

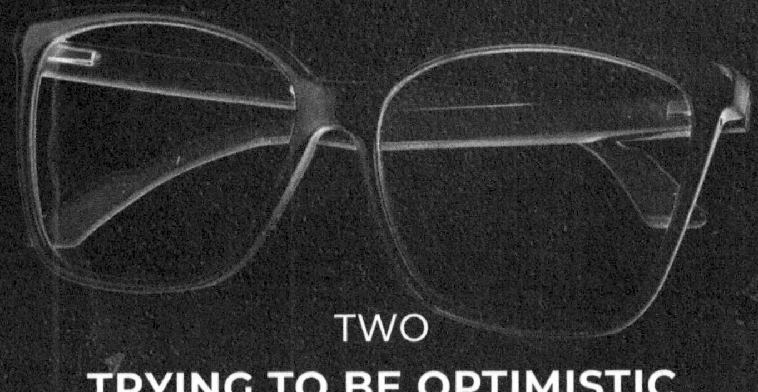

TWO
TRYING TO BE OPTIMISTIC

Elena

GAZING AT MY REFLECTION, I GATHER MY LONG BLOND HAIR AND tie it into a bun before I apply tinted moisturizer, mascara, and strawberry lip balm. I expel a breath. This will have to do. I'm wearing a black three-quarter skirt and a white blouse.

Knock, knock. "Come on, I'm busting to go to the toilet." Jeremy's voice filters through the bathroom door. If these boys are going to live here, sharing one upstairs bathroom with seven people isn't going to work.

I push the door open, and he darts in and starts peeing in the toilet before I can even close the door behind me. I shudder. Gross!

"Tell Cameron I'll see him tonight," he calls out.

Back in my bedroom, I slip my handbag over my shoulder before I leave. I lock my door and go downstairs.

It's quiet compared to last night. When I woke up at two a.m., I could hear their voices and music. Empty pizza boxes and beer bottles and glasses from last night are scattered across the coffee table. I hope this isn't a daily occurrence, but I suspect it might be.

In the kitchen I pour water into a glass and take my anxiety medication out of my bag. I swallow my daily dose: two tablets. I've been on anxiety medication since high school, when I put so much pressure on myself to do well that my hands would shake.

"I've got this," I say, trying to convince myself that I'm confident before I head out the front door.

I walk to my faded yellow Mini Cooper. It's older than me, but despite a few bangs and scratches from my driving, it gets the job done. My seat creaks as I get in and settle while I open the GPS app on my phone. "Don't let me down," I mumble. My GPS says it's a seven-minute drive, but I'm leaving early, in plenty of time before my shift starts at eleven.

My heart beats faster the closer I get to the restaurant. The town's main road runs along the beach. The water is calm, and it lazily laps the shore. I see small shops to my left and palm trees scattered along the sidewalk.

The restaurant is just up ahead. As I approach, a car leaves an angled parking spot nearby. I put on my blinker, and after several attempts and a car horn blasting, I reverse park. When I get out of the car, I see that I parked a little too close to the line for comfort, but I ignore it and make my way to the sidewalk, trying to control my breathing with slow breaths.

The restaurant appears modern, with floor-to-ceiling windows and a deck that wraps around the outside. A black sign with gold lettering proudly displays the name of the restaurant and my new place of employment: Crown Village Seafood Restaurant. It's fine dining, and I hope I'm not out of my depth. I'm not the most graceful person. I think the manager at my last restaurant gave me a good reference to get rid of me. I accidentally broke several plates and glasses. I always apologized, but I'm lucky I kept my job as long as I did.

A Closed sign hangs on the door, but when I knock lightly, a young man appears. He opens the door, and I say, "Hello, I'm Elena. I'm supposed to be starting today." I try to sound confident, though I don't feel it.

The man's eyes roam my body, making me shift uncomfortably. His smile widens when his eyes reach mine. "Hey, sorry," he says and opens the door further. "Come on in. The name's Cameron."

I carefully enter. My stomach rolls like crazy.

"You're more beautiful in person," he quips, and I pause. "I had to check out your Instagram profile," he says casually, and then he laughs when I don't answer. "My father makes me ensure I'm hiring the right people; he can't hire someone whose behavior will reflect poorly on the business. You know . . . our family restaurant's reputation is important."

As I exhale, my shoulders sag an inch. "Of course," I say and smile. He was doing his due diligence for his family's business.

"Come take a seat," Cameron says, glancing at the closest two-seater table.

He sits down opposite me, and I can't help but notice that he's handsome, with brown eyes and hair and a broad smile.

"Thank you for giving me this opportunity. I appreciate it." More than he will know—it allowed me to get out of my hometown.

His eyes light up. "It's my pleasure. About the restaurant, we serve seafood, obviously. It's fine dining, so the customers expect professional service. Your role at the beginning is to bring out food to the designated tables. Simple. I need you to smile and be professional and approachable." His eyes trail me again. "What you're wearing is perfect."

I clasp my hands together and sit up straight, trying not to show how nervous I am.

He takes a menu from the table and passes it to me. "We serve primarily high-quality, locally sourced and sustainable seafood and produce, and our prices match our ethos." He glances down at his watch. "The chefs and waitresses will arrive soon to prepare for lunch. I'll have one girl show you the ropes, and you can shadow her today. If you have any questions, just let me know."

His phone rings and he pulls it from his pocket. "Hey," he answers and puts a finger up at me, signaling he'll be a moment. I nod and give him a small smile before he walks toward the rear of the restaurant and enters a door that I assume leads to the kitchen.

As I wait for him to return, I survey the restaurant. Tables are separated evenly around and ringed with elegant chairs with timber legs and plush fabric seats. The real beauty is the full view of the ocean.

Members of staff come in through the front door; the men smile at me, and a bald one gives me a friendly wave. They head to the back of the restaurant. Women dressed similarly to me walk in, but they pay no attention to me. Not that I'm anyone important, but I was hoping to make a few friends while I'm here.

Cameron's been gone for a while, so I pull my phone out of my bag. When the women start setting up the tables, I stand up to help just as Cameron reappears and the front door opens.

"Mel, good to see you've turned up."

A girl around my age with a short pixie cut walks in. She gives Cameron a big smile, walks to him, and gives him a kiss on the cheek.

I'm surprised at the affection. I hope Cameron doesn't expect that from me.

"Miss me, did you?" she purrs.

"Always," he says playfully, and then he turns toward me. "Elena is new. She's shadowing you today." He turns back to Mel. "Be nice," he says sternly.

That is not an encouraging sign.

Cameron walks away and Mel moves toward me, her eyes scanning me up and down. "I can see why he hired you."

I clear my throat. "Why do you say that?"

"He only hires attractive waitresses." Her eyes drift over me again. "Come with me. I'll show you where to put your things."

As I walk behind her, I notice that she's dressed like me, although her skirt is a lot shorter than mine. I tap her on the shoulder and lower my voice. "I don't have to kiss Cameron on the cheek, do I?" I recoil at the thought.

She laughs. "No, but it'll do you a lot of good to be *very* friendly to him. The tips here are worth putting up with him. I encourage it, though, because I usually get the best shifts when I do."

I've already decided that that won't be happening. I guess I'll have to deal with getting the crappy shifts.

We walk past the tables, then through the large doors and into the kitchen area. Mel puts her bag on a shelf. "Put your bag up here."

As I put my bag away, Mel's phone beeps. She pulls it out, then laughs when she stares at the screen and types.

"Boyfriend?" I ask, making small talk.

She waves me off, then puts her phone away. "No, a guy from this dating app I'm on."

I blink a few times, unsure how to reply. "Cool."

Butterflies perform acrobatics in my stomach as I make every effort to take in Mel's instructions on the details of my job. Cameron was right. It doesn't seem too complicated, and I try to remember table numbers and the menu.

Apart from Cameron watching my every move, my first shift is a blur of friendly faces and the delicious aroma of food wafting through the restaurant. Once the last patron leaves, I help clean the tables and then grab my bag. Cameron leans against the wall close to me, making me take a small step back.

His eyes flick over me before he says, "How was your first shift?"

"Good, thank you."

He smiles. "I'll see you tomorrow at the same time. Can you also work the evening shift tomorrow?"

More shifts, more money. "I sure can. I live with Lucy and the girls. Jeremy said he'll see you tonight."

Cameron's brows lift. "You live with Lucy?"

I nod.

"Looks like we'll be seeing a lot more of each other. Are you coming out to the diner too?" he asks.

I'm not sure how I feel about seeing my boss at my house. "Early night for me tonight. Have fun though."

I follow Mel outside and glance around one last time. "Are there any other staff members I haven't met yet?"

"Only a couple of girls that do casual shifts," Mel answers.

At my last restaurant there was both waiters and waitresses. "Aren't there any waiters?"

She opens the door and we walk out. She flashes me a smile. "You noticed that, huh? Cameron reckons women bring in more customers—therefore, more money—but I think he just likes to perve on us. I saw Cameron's got his eye on you."

A sense of unease twists knots inside of me, despite my attempts to stay optimistic. I don't want any special attention. I want to do what I do best—blend into the background. My introverted self doesn't enjoy going out to socialize. I'm happy being at home reading a book.

A loud rumble makes me jerk, and I pivot to the sound of motorcycles passing us. I count seven black bikes that, even for a person who knows nothing about bikes, look high-end. Their black and chrome parts shine in the sun. The men driving them, who are wearing matching vests, seem scary.

"That's the War Brothers MC," Mel says after they pass us. "They're the hottest men in town." She lets out a long sigh. "What I wouldn't do to become a sweet butt."

I turn around to face her. "What's a sweet butt?"

"The women who are allowed to live there with the men. They help at the clubhouse doing cleaning and cooking, but they're in it for the sex and to live there rent-free. I'm so jealous!"

I'm disturbed by that revelation and realize I grew up very sheltered.

Her phone pings, and she pulls it out and smiles. Her eyes return to mine. "Do you have a boyfriend?"

"No." Henry and I are just friends now. He has always treated me well, but our connection seemed more like a friendship than a romantic relationship.

"Have you thought about setting up a profile on a dating app?" she asks enthusiastically.

I shake my head. "I recently got out of a relationship. I'm not interested. Anyway, aren't the guys on them only after sex and hooking up?"

"No, you can put what you're after on your profile. Everyone's rich here. You have to agree that it would be lovely to go out and be wined and dined for a night. It's whatever you want it to be."

I shrug. "It doesn't interest me." I just moved here. I have next to no experience with guys and the thought sends my heart racing.

She tilts her head. "You're weird, you know that?"

I chuckle. "Yes, I'm well aware." I've always been shy; I can't help it. I live vicariously through the books I read.

"I'll see you tomorrow," she says over her shoulder as she walks away.

"See you then," I reply and walk over to my car.

A new town, a new job, and an unspoken hope for a new beginning.

THREE
THE BET

Axle

Viper, Cash, and I are hanging out at the clubhouse bar. The music is pumping, and one of my favorite bands, Motionless in White, is playing. I join in, singing to the chorus.

"Shit, you sound terrible," Viper says, smirking.

I sing louder just to spite him, using my hand as a microphone. I scream at the end until he throws a dirty tea towel at me and scores a direct hit to my face.

I gag, rip it off, and throw it back at Cash, who's standing behind the bar. "That stinks!"

He laughs. "It shut you up, didn't it?"

Viper's squinting at me. "Can you hear your own voice?"

I nod. "Sure can."

"Then you must hear how shit you sound."

I gasp dramatically. "You must have a hearing problem then," I say to Viper, fighting off a grin.

He shakes his head as he chuckles.

"Did I just hear something dying?" Reaper, the president

of our club, is walking toward us with an expression of disgust on his face, which makes all of us laugh.

"You mean the sound of an angel," I clarify.

"If the angel was being brutally murdered," Demon chimes from the pool table, where he's playing a game with Twitch.

I roll my eyes. "Well, I've got to entertain myself somehow."

The other men return to their conversations. Grace sashays over to me, giving me a flirtatious glance. I groan. Prime example number one of why I'm bored—no more casual sex with the stage-five clinger. I shake my head. "Not now," I call out to her over the music, loud and clear.

She pauses, but then keeps walking toward me while Viper chuckles next to me. I grit my teeth and plaster on a smile, trying not to lose my shit at her.

"Oh, come on, baby," she coos, pushing up her boobs, which are about to burst out of her bra-like top.

She's hot . . . amazing body, but she needs a big fucking wake-up call. We will never be anything but fuck buddies. My nonexistent patience vanishes. I raise my voice and stress, "I said, *not now*."

Her eyes widen. She fakes a tight-lipped smile and retreats.

I blow out a breath. "Fuuuck! I'm trying my best not to be a dick because she's a sweet butt and lives here, but she's making it really fucking difficult."

Viper looks at me with a raised brow. "What's up with you lately?"

"She's in full stage-five-clinger mode. Even started asking me if I would ever get married." I shake my head while Viper laughs.

He cringes. "That's heavy. She realizes she's living at a motorcycle club, right?"

"*Exactly*. I knew I had to stop the casual sex right away. Next she'll be poking holes in condoms, trying to get pregnant."

Viper throws his head back, letting out a loud laugh as Cash asks, "Does anyone want another drink?"

"Another beer," I say.

I thought going for a long ride on my Harley today with all the club members would lift my spirits and calm my restlessness, but it was a temporary fix. "We need to have a massive party here. Spread the word for chicks from nearby towns and girls who recently moved here for college."

"I'm keen," Viper replies, upbeat. "Is that's what's up your ass? You want new pussy?"

I shrug. "This town is pretty small, and we've been through a lot of the women here." A *lot*.

He raises his brow. "What exactly are you after?"

My eyes wander over the women in the clubhouse, and I grimace. "The opposite of them," I say, and tilt my head toward the sweet butts. Vera, Grace, Candy, and Mercedez are dancing to the music and rubbing up against each other.

"I don't want an easy girl. I want someone to keep my interest . . . I want . . ." My lip twitches. "Innocent."

Viper puffs out a breath of air. "Keep dreaming. Have you ever even met a nun?"

I chuckle. "She doesn't have to be a nun."

"Virgins want relationships. Good luck finding one that doesn't."

I don't want a relationship. She doesn't have to be a virgin either. A challenge is what I'm after. Viper has a point. Biker parties aren't the place to find someone like that. But then inspiration strikes. "I'm going to go on one of those dating apps."

Viper's eyes brighten. "That is going to end up being some

great entertainment. You'll have to show me who you find on there."

I pull my phone out and search for dating apps.

One hour later, I've signed up to three. The chiming of message notifications makes my smug grin stretch wide.

"See . . . the ladies flock to me."

Viper shakes his head, trying to smother a smirk. "Not the lady you're after."

My smile vanishes.

"Did you put on your profile that you're a member of a motorcycle club?"

"Yeah, of course I did." It always attracts the ladies.

"Idiot! Delete that part, and don't use any photo of you that shows your cut," he says while pointing at my War Brothers MC vest.

"Do I have to take a picture with my hair parted on the side like a good boy as well?" I say, my voice dripping with sarcasm.

He chuckles. "No, I'm just saying if you want to attract a different type of woman, you're going to have to change it up a bit, at least for the first part, anyway."

This is going to be harder than I thought. I crop one of my photos so that it shows only my head and shoulders and nothing about being in a motorcycle club, and I change my occupation to mechanic. Even though I'm not qualified as one, I'm just as skilled.

Next I browse profiles, choosing women within a two-hour drive from here. I'm not driving any further than that to see them. I want to open the net as wide as possible because I'm sure the women who live here know my face. A few of the women who have matched with me are local. "Nope"—swipe. "Nope"—swipe. I delete their requests.

An hour later, as I'm flicking through the women on the app, I find a pretty little thing with long blond hair and a sweet smile. "Fucking perfect." In her profile picture, she's wearing jeans and a fancy long top. I click on her profile. There's not much information about her. Just that she works in Crown Village at a restaurant. I've never seen her before. I frown when I see she doesn't have any other photos.

"Do you think this one's a catfish?" I ask Viper. I give him my phone.

"Ohhh," he says, amused. "She's hot! You'll never know until you talk to her." He zooms in on the picture and laughs. "You've found your nun."

"Why do you say that?" I ask.

"She's wearing a gold cross around her neck."

Excitement buzzes through me. *Fuck yeah*. That's a sign right there!

I'm halfway through my beer when my phone chimes. When I look down at it, my heart jolts. "She matched me!" I cheer. "If I spend some time with her, that should make Grace leave me alone too. I'm just saying . . . two birds, one stone." Grace can move on to one of my brothers.

Viper throws his head back. "Ha! The only way you're going to get into that pussy is in your dreams!"

I pull at my cut, then mockingly run a hand through my hair like he usually does. "We all can't be as pretty as you."

He laughs. "She looks young and classy. Take another look at her picture! Her clothes cover most of her skin. I'm sure she has a chastity belt on too. I'm telling you—she will never go out with a biker."

The photo of the innocent woman glows from my screen.

"You want to make a bet on that? I guarantee I can get into a relationship with her, and I'll take it one step further and make her fall in love with me." Because I'm pretty sure that's the only way I'll be getting into those sweet panties. I can't help myself. I'm spurred on by the thrill of the gamble and of getting with someone I've never been with before.

Viper's smile widens and his hand shoots out. I grip his hand and shake it. "Easiest money I've ever made," he says confidently.

My eyes tighten. "You're wrong, and I can't wait to wipe that smug smile right off your face."

"Don't forget," he remarks with a cocky smirk, "she probably won't have sex till marriage."

My eyes bulge and I swallow hard. "She better not! That's old school anyway." I wave him off. "No one does that anymore."

"Yeah, they do," he says, and chuckles. "And here's another thought. You'll be talking to her through messages. How's she going to understand your dyslexic ass?"

A sigh escapes me. I'd forgotten about that. I'm going to have to download an autocorrect app on my phone to double check everything I write because I'm terrible at spelling—well, anything related to writing and reading. I'm good at fixing shit, which is why I'm a mechanic.

"I'll work it out. I've never seen her before. Her profile says she lives in Crown Village. She must have just moved here."

He shrugs. "Talk to her and find out."

"Oh, I plan to." I might even get Twitch, our club's tech guy, to stalk her online for me.

FOUR
DATING APP

Elena

Focusing on the glasses of wine on my tray, I stroll to the table that ordered them. *Nearly there . . . .* Someone at a table nearby scoots their chair out in front of me. I gasp, then trip over the chair legs. I stagger and, with a high-pitched clatter, the glasses of red wine shatter on the wooden floor. For a second I seem to regain my balance, but then I fall next to the wine and broken glass.

My face is on fire as I assess the mess. When I look up, everyone in the restaurant is staring at me. "I'm so sorry," I stutter, not sure who I'm apologizing to. "I'll clean it up," I say in a rush. I turn to the customers who ordered the wine. "I'll get you another two glasses."

The woman who pushed out her chair doesn't even apologize—she just turns her nose up at me and walks away. So rude!

Then Cameron is by my side, wearing his customer service smile. "I'll get you your drinks right away," he says to the couple whose drinks are now on the floor. "Can you two clean this up?" he points to Mel and another waitress. Mel's eyes widen and her mouth twists.

"Sorry," I mouth as Cameron grabs my elbow and ushers me away to the kitchen. I close my eyes when he turns to me, waiting to be yelled at.

"Are you okay?" he asks.

I open one eye. I was not expecting that. "Uh . . . yes."

His eyes wander over me, and he smiles wide. "I'm glad."

Guilt pricks me. "I'd better go help them clean it up." I take a step away, but he grasps my elbow again and with his other hand waves it off. "Don't worry about them. I said they can clean it." I glance at the door, then at him. He's the boss, but Mel was scowling at us as we left. She did not look happy.

AFTER OUR SHIFT, MEL AND I TAKE SOME LEFTOVER FOOD IN containers and go to the beach to eat it. Sitting on a chair, I slurp up my noodles. "This seafood marinara is to die for."

Mel smiles. "I love every dish on the menu."

"If I didn't work there, I'd never be able to afford it," I point out, remembering the eye-watering prices.

"Cameron has taken a liking to you," she teases. "You might be stealing my shifts." Her voice is carefree, but I'm not fully convinced she means it.

"No," I say as I shake my head. "I just started. He probably felt bad for me. I embarrassed myself in front of everyone." I take another bite.

She giggles. "You certainly did."

I flinch.

"Luckily, it's not carpet," she points out.

"I agree." It would have left a lovely stain.

"I heard you live with Lucy and her sheep," Mel says.

I pause. My eyes widen at her nasty comment. "I live with Lucy and her friends, yes. Do you know them?"

"People get to know each other quickly in this town. Cameron is always saying how hot they are. Were they bitches to you?"

I slowly shake my head. "The opposite. They've been friendly since I arrived."

She frowns. "I thought they'd be like the mean popular girl group from school, you know."

Well, this is awkward. "Not at all."

She shrugs. "I'd say they talk about you behind your back then because you're so . . ."

My lips press into a line. I'm quite sure I have no interest in hearing what she's got to say next. "Because I'm a bit of a nerd." I finish her sentence for her in the nicest possible way.

"Yeah . . . like night and day opposites. Soooo . . ." she says, peering at the ground, then back at me. "I may have done something . . . to, you know, help you meet new people."

My stomach drops. I don't like the sound of that. "What did you do?"

She winces. "Can I have your phone to show you?"

My breathing speeds up as I cautiously offer her my phone. I try to think why she would need my phone, but I can't think of anything.

"Now . . . don't be mad at me . . ."

"O-kaaay," I say.

She passes me the phone. I frown when I see a picture of myself that was taken when my parents and I went out to dinner for my birthday last year. As I scroll down, it hits me. "You made a dating profile for me?" I screech. "I'm deleting it now!" I'm horrified.

She grins a little. "Give it a chance. Live a little. You should consider meeting new people."

I look more closely. She has Elena as my profile name; "Just moved to Crown Village, where I'm working at a restaurant. I'm looking to meet new people" is the bio.

"What if my parents see this?" I ask, then flinch. Why should I care what they think?

She gives me an odd glance. "I didn't realize you were fourteen years old."

Annoyance simmers. "I grew up in a strict family." I just moved here. It's hard to click my fingers and change my thoughts after years of worrying about my parents' opinions. I'll be defaulting to that for a while.

"And you still let your parents dictate what you do?" She chuckles.

"I don't get it . . ." I stare at her, confused. "Why would you do this? You're already on the app, and you hardly know me."

Her pout makes me think I shouldn't have said that. "I was trying to do a *nice* thing."

Oh dear. I think I offended her. I swallow down my irritation. I bring my phone to my face again. "Where'd you get this photo from?"

"I got it from your Instagram account. See, fifteen guys want to connect with you already."

I blink slowly. I'm waiting for her to say she's joking, but she doesn't. "You didn't . . . .?" is all I can say because I'm reeling.

"You need it. Meet some new guys. Have fun." She glances away. "I may have already swiped yes on one of them."

My jaw drops. It just gets worse. "Who?"

"A guy called Axle."

I scoff. "What an absurd name."

"I've been on the app for a while, and I've never seen his profile. He recently joined, like you. He's from Crown Village, and he's so sexy. Trust me, you want to talk to him."

"Well, why don't you talk to him then?"

She pauses, then says, "It's my gift to you. I've heard he's good fun." Her critical gaze runs over me again, but then she smiles. "You're not getting married to the guy. Just talk to him."

"How do you know him, and why do you say he's fun?" I ask.

"I've seen him around. It's a small town." She takes a moment before she says, "He sticks to himself and his group of friends."

"So he's not some frat guy?"

She laughs. "No, definitely not . . . quite the opposite."

The message icon at the top of the screen shows the number one above it. I hold my breath and let my finger hover over it for a second before I press on it.

Axle

> Hey, how are you doing?

I just stare at the message.

"See . . . it's not the end of the world," Mel points out.

I get out of the message and click on his profile. He's very handsome, and I'm sure he knows it. Short brown hair and a beard. His profile is minimal, like mine. It says he's a mechanic and, according to his bio, "looking for someone special." I melt a little at that. Maybe there are nice guys on the app after all.

I can't deny I'm curious to talk to him. No one as handsome as him has ever shown an interest in me. "But I'm not looking for another relationship," I say. I shove my phone back in my bag with more force than necessary. He must have gotten my profile mixed up with someone else's.

When I get back to the house, it's quiet. Everyone must be at class. After a shower, I lie on the bed. My stomach churns. I glance down at my bag beside the bed. I'm itching to grab my phone. My fingers tap on the bed until I can't resist the urge any longer and give in to the temptation. I pull out my phone and with a deep breath, I unlock it and tap on the dating app.

I look at Axle's profile picture once more. I should just delete the app, but I can't stop myself from responding to his message:

I'm good, thank you. How are you?

I stare at the screen and place my phone on the night-stand, face down. I can't believe I just did that. I replied to a stranger. I run my hand over my face. Mel could be right, even though it's out of character for me. I should step out of my comfort zone and try to make friends.

My phone buzzes on the table. Here goes nothing . . .

Fantastic now that I'm talking to you 😊

I stare blankly. I start typing and then delete it.

You're beautiful babe. Your profile says you just moved here. Are you enjoying it?

My face heats.

The people are nice.

I'm nice.

I laugh. I bet he's *nice* to all women.

How old are you?

Early twenties. How old are you?

Ha . . . don't give too much away now. Early twenties.

I'm getting banter and sarcasm vibes.

What brings a pretty little thing like you onto a dating website?

I decide not to go with the truth.

I want to make some new friends.

I'm an amazing friend. You're so lucky you replied to me.

I giggle.

Someone is full of himself.

Only stating facts, babe. I'm funny, I'm sexy as fuck, I'll listen to all your problems, and I'll be your shoulder to cry on. Trust me, we are going to be good friends.

I smile. Maybe the app isn't too bad after all.

FIVE
HALF-TRUTHS

Axle

ALL THE MEN ARE OUTSIDE CLEANING THEIR MOTORCYCLES. After replacing the back tire on mine, I hear a chuckle, then peer up to see Cash looking at me, amused.

"What?" I ask him, wondering why he has that stupid look on his face.

"Didn't you just replace the back tire?"

A smile curves across my lips. "Yes, I did." I love doing power skids, burnouts, and wheelies. It's who I am. The adrenaline rush is pure ecstasy.

"Are you ever going to grow out of your daredevil ways?" he asks, though the smile pulling at his lips suggests he already knows the answer to that question.

"Never! You should know that by now."

Cash and I spent years in the military together. It's how we met. He knows me well. I'm always doing reckless things, especially on my motorcycle. I've never cared about my safety —I'm always searching for the next thrill.

After cleaning my motorcycle, I step aside. "What a sexy beast," I say.

"Mine's sexier," says Viper.

I laugh loudly. "You wish . . . My exhaust is louder." My phone chimes inside my pocket. "Oh, look out, it's the wife," I say, ensuring Viper can hear.

He scoffs. "Oh fuck off!"

"It's true," I say smugly, then glance at Elena's profile picture again. Dayum, she's hot. She's much too innocent for me, but I don't give a shit. "Check it out yourself then."

Viper steps over to me and snatches my phone. I see him swiping and going through the messages.

He laughs. "You sound like an absolute pussy. Though I guess that's the point." He keeps swiping. "Jesus, you have been talking a lot. Did you ask her how church was?"

"Yeah, I did actually . . ."

His eyes flash wide. "You didn't?"

I chuckle. "No, but I told her I liked her necklace. I told you Viper—you're losing our bet."

"We'll see," he says. "Are we still organizing the party here?"

I nod sharply. "We sure are."

"What did the messages say?" Cash asks as he steps toward us. The whole MC knows of my bet with Viper. I've been bragging about my charm to anyone who will listen. Viper's going to lose. I'm going to make sure of it.

"She just moved here," Viper answers. "She works at a restaurant and enjoys reading." Viper's smile is huge. "She might be able to teach you."

"Really funny, aren't you?" I say sarcastically to the prick.

"Yep," he says. "She's into happily ever afters . . . you're going to break her virgin heart."

Virgin? Shiiit. I don't know whether it would be a good thing or a bad thing . . . not that I've asked yet. A weird sensation flickers through my chest. Perhaps it's guilt, but it leaves as quickly as it came.

Viper carries on reading, then peers back at Cash. "Axle makes a lame joke about him only reading motorcycle magazines. The nun has a sister blah blah blah. Just basic shit." Viper passes me back my phone. "The messages mean nothing."

"It's only been a few days," I tease. She's eating up all the attention I throw at her. This is surely going to be a breeze.

"Until she finds out you're a biker," he mocks.

I raise my brow. "That could be my way in. Good girls love bad boys."

Elena

WE HAVEN'T STOPPED MESSAGING. AS SOON AS I FINISH WORK, I'm back on my phone. He's addicting and charming. I smile stupidly at the screen.

Axle

> Where do you work, so I can come and say hi?

I rub my arm. Messaging and meeting up are two very different things.

> I hardly know you.

> Well, then you can get to know me 😊

> I want to see your pretty face and I'm dying to see your smile.

I blush. If this is how I'm behaving over messages, I could only imagine how hard it would be if I met him. He's a lot, but I can't stop myself from messaging back.

> Where do you work, then?

> I'll tell you when you tell me.

I shake my head.

> You're cheeky!

> You have no idea. 😉 At least give me your phone number, so I don't have to message you on this app. C'mon, I want to hear your voice.

I snicker as I stroll from my car toward work. I swiftly reply.

> You give me yours first and I'll decide if I want to talk to you. I've got work. Talk to you later.

I put my phone away.

"Hey," Mel says as she falls into step with me.

"Hey," I reply cheerfully.

She tilts her head and points at me, her mouth gaping open. "You've been talking to Axle, haven't you?" She doesn't allow me to reply. "Tell me all about it! I want details!"

I can't help but smile back. "He's really nice, very charming."

She scrunches her nose. "What did you just say? Did you

say he's nice?"

I inch back, surprised at her reaction. "Yes, he is. He wants to meet me, but I've just started talking to him." I can't stop the thought of my parents' disapproval if they knew I was considering meeting up with a stranger.

Her eyes dart away before she glances back at me. "Did you want me to meet up with him first to, you know"—she smiles—"check he's decent."

I give her an odd look. "I thought you have met him?"

She shakes her head. "Only seen him and heard about him from others."

"Um, no, thank you. I haven't decided what I'm going to do yet."

We walk inside the restaurant, put our bags away, and put on our aprons. Cameron walks toward us, his eyes sparkling. "Good to see you, ladies."

I give him a tight smile and squirm under his gaze as his eyes run up and down our bodies.

Mel steps to him and kisses his cheek. "Hey," she says in a flirty tone, but his eyes stay on me.

"Hello," I reply to Cameron. I need the money, and apart from his wandering eyes, he's a kind boss and he gave me an opportunity to leave my hometown. He could be a lot worse, and I've made a friend in Mel.

"How's it living at home with Lucy and the gang?" he asks with a smirk and a raised brow.

"They're out a lot at college during the day and partying at night, so we haven't crossed paths often, considering I'm working."

He chuckles. "They sure love to party. Study hard, play hard. You should come to one of the parties. It'll be fun."

I draw back. "I'm not a big party person." Or a big socializing person. My kind of big night is staying up late to finish a book.

His eyes flash and his smile widens. "Well, we'll just have to bring the party to you. I'll get the girls to organize a party at your house."

Oh fantastic! I force a smile, but deep down I'm dreading it. At least at someone else's party I can leave when I want to. If it's at our house, I'll have to lock myself inside my room. "Oh, you don't have to worry about throwing a party for me."

When he leaves to go talk to the other waitresses, Mel leans in close to me. "I told you. He's got his eyes on you."

I put that uncomfortable thought to the back of my mind.

She laughs. "He's flirty and sometimes can get a little handsy, but just think of the money."

My head whips to her, my eyes bulging. "Handsy?" I squeak.

She brushes me off with a wave. "Don't stress. It's only minor touches; like, he doesn't grab my ass or tits or anything. Just sly feels—like, he brushes against me, stands too close and touches my hip and stuff. Nothing you can't handle. Trust me, I've had worse."

My breathing and heartbeat have accelerated. I've got to find a way to be polite to Cameron while ensuring I don't flirt back to provoke him and I'm firm if he does touch me. I can't lose this job. I don't want to go back home. I'm learning and getting a bit more confident in the position each day.

I work hard during my shift, and when I finish and am walking out the door, I pull out my phone and see Axle's number in the dating app messages. I'm in two minds about it. What if he ends up being a stalker or some guy who won't leave me alone? Then he has my number. I guess I could block it.

I wish I had my sister, Ava, or someone apart from Mel to talk to. I want to talk to Ava so bad . . . but I'm not sure if she'd even answer my call. We used to be so close, but everything changed when she met her husband. I need someone to talk some sense into me because I'm clearly not in my right mind.

When I arrive at home, I dash up the stairs. I shower and then lie on my bed. The reason I moved here was because I needed a change. My life never moved forward in my old town. My heart surges as I try to decide whether to call Axle.

I heave a sigh. *Just do it!* I give in to my intrusive thoughts, pick up my phone, and dial the number.

"Hello," a husky voice answers. There's loud music in the background, and I freeze. My mouth opens, but nothing comes out. It gets quiet. "Hello . . . Elena?"

"Hi."

He chuckles. "About time you called," he says playfully.

I can't help but smile. "I was at work." Did he miss talking to me? I shake my head. Don't be ridiculous.

"Hold on a sec, I need to go to my room." It makes me wonder where he lives and if he's living in shared accommodation like me.

There's a shuffling sound of movement, then a bang, as if a door was slammed closed. The music quietens. "Are we going on a date tomorrow?" he asks boldly.

I choke on nothing. "A date?"

"Yeah . . . a date . . . with me. Come on, I know you want to," he purrs.

He's a massive flirt. I'm in way over my head.

"Does your silence mean yes?"

I chuckle nervously. "I've only just started talking to you. I can't meet you yet."

"Why? We're friends, remember? Friends spend time together." He pauses. "Are you too good for me? That's not very nice, you know."

I huff. "I am not too good for anyone." Damn it, a wave of guilt washes over me. "I'm a nice person."

"Prove it!"

Still uncertain, I say, "I'll think about it." It's a big risk on my part.

"I'll take that as a yes," he's quick to respond.

I gape. "I never—"

"See you tomorrow, Elena," he cuts in, his tone seductive. He hangs up and I'm left staring at my phone. He must be joking . . . He doesn't know where I work.

I put my phone down. Surely, he won't find me. I pick up my reading glasses and book and open it at the bookmark. I try not to think of Axle, but my thoughts keep drifting back to him.

SIX

SURPRISE!

Elena

MY PHONE CHIMES, WAKING ME UP. I GROGGILY BRING IT TO MY face and see a message from Axle.

Axle

Hey Babe, I hope you had a great sleep. I'm excited to see you today 😉

I shift and sit up.

Morning. I think you have me confused with another woman.

I'm not talking to anyone else. Are you talking to another guy?

My cheeks flush slightly, and a soft smile tugs at the corners of my lips.

No, I'm not.

I've been ignoring the requests on the dating app, and I haven't talked to anyone else apart from the people I live and work with.

Great! What time are we meeting? When's your lunch break?

He's persistent.

How do you know I'm even working?

You always seem to be working.

I need to get to know you more before I meet you.

Even though I'm curious, I'm not ready . . . my shy self may never be ready. I go back to the dating app again and tap on his profile. Short, thick brown hair, trimmed beard, full lips . . . and that jaw. He's so handsome. In his photo he's wearing a leather jacket.

After changing into my workout clothes, I pull out my yoga mat, unroll it, and begin breathing work and stretches. Then I select the yoga app on my phone and begin following the directions of the voice on the app. I should take the time before and between my shifts to explore the town. I make a mental note to start tomorrow. I need to get out of my comfort zone, even though just the thought of it makes me queasy.

When I finish doing yoga, I shower and head downstairs for breakfast. It sounds quiet again. I guess they're sleeping off their hangovers. I woke up at three to loud voices. Everyone sounded drunk, and they mentioned the word *party*, so I assume they had just gotten home from one.

Downstairs the girls are sitting on the couches. They're in

their pajamas, huddled under blankets, their hair ruffled. I try not to laugh at them. "Big night?"

Lucy nods at me slowly. "My head hurts."

"At least you weren't up vomiting," says Lia, who appears to be a pretty shade of white.

"You should come with us next time," says Cindy.

Jasmine laughs. "She won't go to a party." Jasmine is correct.

"I seem to work the evening shifts anyway." Not that I would. So many people drunk together in a small space . . . *no thank you.* I gaze at them. They look sick, and I'd prefer not to waste a whole day being hungover.

"We'll make Cameron give you a night off," Lia replies. "How's it working with him?"

I pause. "He's friendly." I'm a little uneasy with him, but he could just be overly flirty, and that's just the way he is, while I'm socially awkward, anxious, and overthinking everything. I smooth my skirt. "I'd better get going to work. I'll see you girls later." With a round of byes, I'm out the door and off to work.

I reverse park outside. You'd think that after parking the same way every day I'd get better at it. I absolutely am not. Inside the restaurant Mel and Cameron are talking by the counter toward the back. She's straightening his shirt. He shifts his gaze from Mel to me and his face lights up. It's only me. I have no idea why he seems to get excited.

"My girl Elena," he says with a bright smile.

My shoulders stiffen at the comment. I smile at both of them, say hello, and slip through the kitchen doors. As I'm putting my bag away and getting ready for my shift, I turn to find Cameron standing behind me. I jerk back.

He grasps my upper arms. "I didn't mean to startle you."

"That's okay," I reply, though my heart thuds in my chest.

"I got a message from Lia this morning. Am I working you too hard?"

My face falls. She messaged him. "Oh no," I stumble over my words. "They said I should go to a party with them," I rush out. "I told them I work at night, but I didn't say you worked me too hard." It was my excuse to stop everyone from asking me. I didn't know it would backfire.

He laughs. "I'm joking. I'll give you this Friday off. You can come with us. The parties here are fun. You're missing out."

Dread fills me. I don't like parties, and it doesn't sit well with me. He's giving me the night off only so that I can spend it with him and his friends. I glance away and fix my ponytail. "Maybe," I say offhandedly.

When Cameron walks away, Mel comes over. "Did Cameron say you're not working Friday?" she asks quietly.

"He did."

"I love my weekends off. You can work mine if you want."

I'm looking forward to my day off. She must notice my expression because she says, "Don't worry about it."

"No, no, I'll do it." It's an excuse for not going to the party, I guess.

She smiles. "Awesome. Thanks. You don't want to go to a party with them anyway. All they do is get drunk and hook up."

That's why I don't want to go. "Can you show me around town after our shift?" If someone else shows me, then I shouldn't get lost. I'm hopeless with directions.

"I'm busy . . . Maybe another time?"

Disappointment hits me, but I smile anyway. "Yeah, perhaps next time." I really have to meet more people.

The lunch rush is busy. I haven't stopped. Fortunately, no glasses were shattered. I'm wiping a table when I hear the front door open. The room goes quiet.

"Oh. My. God!" Mel says in a high-pitched voice. Before I have time to look up, she rushes to my side, grabs my shoulder, and gives it a shake. "It's him!"

I frown. "Him who?"

"It's Axle!"

Suddenly, I can't breathe. I freeze as all the air is sucked out of my lungs in one big breath. *How did he find me?* I briefly gather courage before stealing a glance at him. He saunters in, surveys the restaurant. His face is passive until his eyes find me. A broad grin spreads across his face. With a confident stride, he approaches. My heart pounds with such force that it might crack a rib.

Axle checks me out with no subtlety whatsoever. He's wearing dark jeans, a fitted white shirt, and a vest. This is the part where I should run, but my limbs are frozen solid and my feet are bolted to the floor. Anxiety courses through my veins.

Axle stands right before me. I swallow hard and stare up at his big hazel eyes and crooked smile. I'm so small compared to him.

"Don't I get a hug?" he asks cheekily, with a raised brow. "We're good friends after all."

I'm trying to smile, but I think it might look more like a grimace. *He's flirting. Eek!*

He steps closer and leans in, and the scent of pine and cedar washes over me. His hot breath makes goosebumps travel up my arms. "You have no reason to fear me. I don't bite . . ." He pauses. "Well, I do, but only if you want me to."

A shiver rolls through me and my jaw drops, hitting the floor with a thump because . . . he did not just say that. "How did you find me?" I squeak, finally finding my words.

He chuckles. "It wasn't difficult."

"I'm Mel," a seductive voice comes from beside me.

I forgot she was standing there. As I look out over the

restaurant, I realize that all eyes are on us, and my cheeks redden.

"Axle," he says to her with a chin lift.

I've never seen Mel smile so wide.

"I was hoping to order," he says before he glances back at me.

"We have a seat available right by the window. The best view in the restaurant," Mel's quick to respond.

"He's not staying." The words seem to fall from my mouth. I flinch. I didn't mean to say that aloud. He's caught me off guard, and I'm a blabbering mess.

He raises his brow, his smile wide. "I want to spend some time at the place you work to convince you to go out on a date with me. So, yes, I am eating in."

I shake my head and lower my voice. "No, you're not. I'm working."

"Is everything okay over here?" Cameron asks quietly. He stands to the side, alternating between looking at Axle and the floor. He seems scared of Axle. Should I be too?

"He's leaving," I say at the same time Axle says, "I'm ordering."

"This way," Mel says and ushers him toward a table. I shake my head at her. Why isn't she listening to me?

Axle says, "I want *Elena* as my waitress."

"Of course," Mel answers and makes her way over to me.

"I heard him," I say before she repeats what he said.

He's just like any other customer. I slowly walk over to him and put on my best customer service smile and play the part. "Are you ready to order?" I keep my tone professional.

His eyes scan me. "I would like to order," he purrs, "but I don't think what I want is on the menu."

I stare at him with bulging eyes. My face burns furiously. Oh my goodness! The confidence and cocky attitude are unlike anything I've ever had to deal with before.

He fights a smile, but his eyes are dancing with mischief. He's enjoying the effect he has on me. I have no idea what I expected, but he is tenfold the personality and I'm struggling to cope. Hell, I can barely talk. I just stare at him like an idiot.

"What do you recommend?" he asks as he glances down at the menu.

"The seafood marinara is good." But I should have answered with, "The food tastes horrible. You should leave because I'm shocked and embarrassed that you found me, and the whole restaurant is staring at us, and my boss is watching our every move." I momentarily close my eyes. I hope I don't get in trouble from my boss for Axle coming here.

Axle bops his head. "I'll have that then."

"Would you like something to drink?"

"A cola, thank you, *Elena*."

I give him a tight nod and bolt through the restaurant and to the kitchen, where I give the chefs the order and take deep breaths.

"You are so lucky!" Mel says loudly.

"Shhh!" I say, not wanting the whole restaurant to hear.

"You lied to me. I thought you weren't meeting him."

"I didn't lie. I don't know how he found me. All I mentioned was that I worked at a restaurant, nothing more."

Cameron walks toward us with narrowed eyes. "What's a War Brothers Motorcycle Club member doing in my restaurant?"

"What are you talking about?" I ask. "I didn't see one."

Mel laughs. "You didn't see Axle's club vest?"

The vest. I cover my face with my hands. He's in a motorcycle club. The situation just went from bad to worse. My next thought is that he doesn't look like a scary biker. He's all charm and crooked smiles.

I drop my hands and give Mel a pointed stare. "Why didn't you tell me?" She had to have known.

She giggles. My lips press into a thin line. I'm seeing nothing funny about this.

"Do you know him?" Cameron asks accusingly.

I flinch. "I don't *know him* know him." I'm pretty sure that didn't make sense, but I'm going with it.

Cameron's lip curls. "Are you dating him?"

"No," I'm quick to answer.

He nods sharply at me. "Good. He's nothing but trouble. I don't want him in my restaurant again. He'll scare away our customers!"

Mel rubs Cameron's back. "It's okay. He's by himself, just having lunch."

"I don't want criminals in my restaurant," he says, then turns to me. "You should be more careful who you make friends with in this town."

When Cameron leaves, I'm left wondering why he seems to dislike Axle so much. "Is he a criminal?" I ask Mel.

She shrugs. "Not that I know of." Not quite the answer I was after. "He's a good type of trouble," she says, and winks. "And you need to take one for the team."

I stare at her confused. "Huh . . . what team?"

She points at each of us in turn. "We're a team. You're friends with Axle, so you can introduce me to all the members of the club. I've wanted to for years."

She's rushing things. I've only just started talking to Axle, and I literally just met him, but yes, he certainly is trouble.

I roll my shoulders back, gather myself, go to the bar, and pour him a cola. I sneak a quick glance. Yep, he's still staring at me. I gaze at him, shake my head, and deliver his drink. As I hand it to him, our fingers briefly touch, making me inhale sharply. Judging by the delight in his eyes, it was intentional.

He takes a sip, and then asks, "When does your shift finish?"

Him asking to see me outside of work makes my pulse quicken. "Why do you ask?"

"Why are you so defensive? I thought we were friends."

Is that what we are? "You turned up at my work."

"I told you I'd see you today," he teases.

"I thought you were joking!"

He tuts. "You shouldn't have assumed. Oh, I get it."

I study him, puzzled. "Get what?"

"You realized I'm a biker, and now you want nothing to do with me."

My lips press into a thin line. I know nothing about bikers. The unknown is what makes me feel uneasy.

"Who told you? Was it the boss who wants to bang you or the chick who wants to bang me?"

I look around. "Shhh! Keep your voice down." What he said irks me. "My boss does not want to bang me," I whisper-yell.

Axle cackles. "Trust me, he does."

I just shake my head. He's impossible.

Mel arrives at the table. "Here you go, your seafood marinara." She puts his plate in front of him, giving him a wink before she goes. She seems keen on him and the MC.

Axle digs his fork into the noodles. "I told you she wants to bang me," he says with a smirk before taking a bite.

I think he's right, which makes me wonder why Mel told me to talk to him. "She was the one who created the dating account. I wouldn't have talked to you if it wasn't for her."

With a thoughtful look, he asks, "Really? Are you free tomorrow?"

"I'm working," I say.

"What about after work?"

I bite my lip. "I'm busy."

"Yeah, you'll be busy."

I watch him curiously while he lounges in his chair.

"You'll be busy going on a date with me."

A laugh breaks out from my lips. "And if I say no?"

He shrugs. "I'll turn up here every day until you say yes." He peers over my shoulder. "Your boss isn't going to like that." He chuckles. "Though pissing him off every day will be amusing."

I know Axle will keep returning. "I don't think you're welcome back here at the restaurant."

His hazel eyes flash with amusement. "He'll never say it to my face."

I glance back at my boss, who abruptly looks away and walks back into the kitchen. I think Axle's right.

"I'll come get you. Tomorrow, before you start your lunch shift, then. Let's say nine?"

I shake my head, the collar of my shirt suddenly feeling too tight around my neck.

His eyes light up at the challenge. He leans in closer to me and looks into my eyes as he says, "Well, you better book me this table for tomorrow."

I don't have any other options. He'll keep turning up at my work. Emotions battle inside of me—excitement, anxiety, and curiosity. It's only in the morning. "I'll think about it. Now I'd better get back to work. I can't lose my job. I only just started here."

While I continue to collect plates and cutlery from other tables, I steal a brief glimpse back at him. He's still staring at me as I head into the kitchen.

After I set the plates near the sink, Mel is beside me once more. "What have you two been talking about?"

I don't have anyone else I can talk to about this. "He asked me out on a date."

She inches back. "Axle doesn't date." Her tone suggests she doesn't believe me.

"He said a date. I'm just repeating what he said."

She pouts. "Maybe he just meant spending time together."

I shrug. "Probably."

"Did you say you were going to have sex with him?"

"No!" I shriek, offended. Does she honestly believe I would pimp myself out to spend time with a guy?

She rests her hand on her hip and glances away, lost in thought. I step around her, only to be met with Cameron.

"How long's he staying for?" Cameron asks sternly.

I blink at him. What is everyone's problem? "I don't know. I gather until he's finished his meal."

"He's finished his meal, and he's asked for *his* waitress."

I wipe my hands on my apron. "I'll go see him now." Then I step around Cameron, feeling both his and Mel's narrowed eyes on me as I leave the kitchen. I know I'm new to the town, but their reactions have me wondering why they have such intense reactions to Axle.

"Are you finished?" I ask. Axle's plate is empty—spotless, in fact. Did he lick the bowl clean?

He slowly nods. "I am."

"The restaurant closes in the next thirty minutes." As in hint hint, nudge nudge, please don't get me into trouble with my boss.

"I'm staying until *you* finish."

I stare at Axle. He chuckles. "And when you start work tomorrow, I'll be here for lunch." He peers behind me. "And dinner." He inches forward, closer to me. "Every day, until you go on a date with me."

I close my eyes. I need this job. When I open them, he looks smug, like he knows he'll follow through. Any girl in my position would have already accepted.

"One date," I warn, though excitement shoots through me.

He rises to his full height, and I have to take a step back because he's so close and much taller than me. The combination of cologne and leather is divine. I peer up. He cups my chin with one hand, making me take a deep breath. "See you tomorrow, *Elena.*"

My knees nearly buckle at his sexy, deep tone.

As he's walking out, I realize I can't have some stranger come to my house, especially one who's in a motorcycle club. "I'll meet you here at work," I yell out in a rush of words.

He pauses and looks over his shoulder, the smug smile back in full force. "I'll pick you up from *your* home."

"No, I'll meet you here," I object.

"I'm picking you up from your home, end of discussion."

I open my mouth to argue.

"Uh," he says, "I know where you live."

I blink in disbelief. "How can you possibly know that?" He just met me, and I've just moved here. It's not like I have friends he could have asked.

"I have my connections," he says with a wink. He swaggers aways while I stand still, dumbfounded.

A shiver rolls through my body. What just happened? How did I end up getting conned into going on a date?

"What happened?" Mel asks.

"I'm *apparently* going out on a date with him."

"You sure he said the word *date*?"

Annoyance bubbles up. "You know, you're really not helping my already low self-esteem." I take Axle's plate and walk to the kitchen, Mel following close behind.

"Sorry, the Axle I've heard about is different from the one I've seen today." She places her hand on my arm. "Good for you, getting out there and meeting new people."

I flash her a faint smile, even though I'm terrified about tomorrow.

After our shift, we step out of the restaurant and go our

separate ways. "Good luck for tomorrow," Mel calls out over her shoulder.

I'll need it!

I drive the short distance home and park outside. When I get into my room, I call my parents, needing to hear a familiar voice.

"Hello," my mother answers.

"Hey, Mom."

"Oh, so you haven't forgotten about us?"

They could have called me to check how I was, but I dismiss it. "I thought you'd like to know I've settled in well. The people I live with are—"

"I still can't believe you live with random people. I bet they're doing drugs and drinking, and God knows what else. Are *you* drinking?"

It's not like I could afford to rent a house here by myself. Sharing a house was my only option. "No, they aren't doing drugs." Well, not that I know of. "And no, I haven't been drinking. I've just been working."

"You know you act like who you hang around, so I hope you're making responsible decisions with people you meet there."

I flinch. I've always been one to believe in the good in the world. I strive to be a positive person and be kind to people who are good to me. "Everyone's been nice to me. I'm getting more comfortable in my job too. I get a view of the beach every time I'm at work."

"Oh, Elena, it's waitressing. It's not hard."

Heaviness weighs on me. There's no need to be nasty. "I'm going to bed; I've had a big day. Say hi to Dad for me."

After I finish the call, I grab a grilled cheese sandwich. I'm left wondering what we'll do tomorrow. Where will Axle take me? Nine in the morning is early, so it can't be too bad . . . Well, I hope so, for my sake.

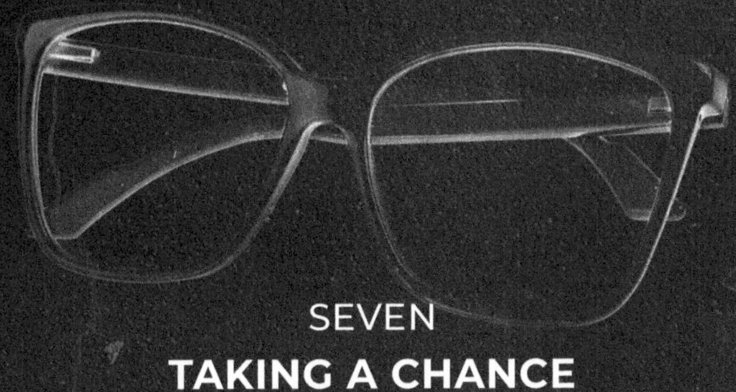

<h1 style="text-align:center">SEVEN
TAKING A CHANCE</h1>

Elena

My mouth is dry . . . Sahara Desert dry. I'm outside on the front porch, pacing. I run my hands over my jeans, up, down, up, down. It's only a date . . . but did Axle mean it's a date like let's hang out or a *date* date? Imagine if my parents or anyone at home discovered I was going on a date with a biker. This is borderline insane. I should just message him to cancel.

"Uh . . . are you okay?"

The voice makes me jump. Lucy and Cindy are at the door with their bags over their shoulders. "I'm okay," I say with fake confidence.

"You sure?" Lucy asks with a raised brow. "It doesn't seem like it."

"Hmmm . . ." Because I'm not okay—I'm low-key terrified. "It's early for you two, isn't it?" They usually sleep the day away.

"We have assignments coming up," Lucy answers. "The

library is quiet, but the real question is, what are you doing?" Suspicion lines her voice.

The thunderous roar of a motorcycle gets louder. My heart thumps harder the closer it gets. Both girls are staring down our street. I turn to see Axle pulling up in front of our house. I used to think that men on motorcycles were scary, but Axle has changed my mind. His personality is anything but scary.

Axle turns his bike off and swings his leg over it. When he gazes at me, there's a wicked smile on his face. I'm getting the impression that it's his signature grin. The girls gasp behind me, and I don't blame them. He is all man and a far cry from my ex-boyfriend and Lucy's boyfriend.

I take hesitant steps toward him as he strides toward me.

"Elena," he says with outstretched arms.

I'm conflicted, both scared and fascinated by him. He must see my apprehension, because he says, "Don't look at me with those eyes."

I shake my head. "Like what?"

"Like I'm some sort of serial killer luring you onto my bike."

That makes me smile.

He grins. "Much better."

I like how he puts me at ease.

"Have you had breakfast, babe?"

I enjoy being called babe a little too much for my liking. "No, I haven't," I reply shyly. It's not like I could eat, knowing I was spending time with him.

"There's a good café in town you'll like. Have you been on a motorcycle before?"

My eyes widen. Why didn't I realize I would be riding with him on his bike?

"I'll take that as a no," he replies, filling the silence for me. He wraps an arm around my shoulders. I tense up a bit, despite the soothing warmth and the enticing scent of his cologne.

"You'll love it," he says as we walk to his motorcycle. It's black and chrome, and it looks fast.

"What if I fall off?" This is me, the clumsiest person on earth. I step out of his hold. He frowns. "This isn't a good idea," I mumble.

"Scared of enjoying yourself, huh?"

The amusement in his voice irritates me, and I narrow my eyes at him. "No," I clip out defensively.

He straddles his bike. "Well . . . get on then," he says, passing me the helmet.

"Okay," I reply, but my breathing is chaotic and I'm silently freaking out. I slip the helmet on and do up the straps under my chin. I peer around his bike. "Where's your helmet?"

"You're wearing it."

I start to unbuckle the helmet. "You can have it back."

"Elena, keep the damn helmet on. You're precious cargo. Now stop making excuses and get on my bike."

"Bossy," I murmur under my breath, though guilt about his safety makes my stomach roll. I fumble onto the bike behind him.

He turns his head. "You're going to have to *actually* touch me. Put your arms around me, hold on to me tight. Keep your legs away from the exhaust and lean when I do."

Simple instructions . . . I'm sure I'll mess it up somehow. The engine roars to life, startling me as I shift slightly in my seat. "You have nothing to worry about," he shouts over the engine. Easy for him to say. I'm the one risking my life on a death trap with a stranger I've just met. Oh, times have changed.

I inhale deeply, allowing the air to calm my nerves. I firmly wrap my arms around him, and I can feel the defined muscles of his abs through his shirt. When I press my cheek against his back, a sense of warmth flows through me at being so close to him.

I catch a glimpse of my roommates, who are staring at me with bulging eyes, their mouths agape. This whole situation is a shock to me too. I glance at the sky, uttering a prayer to protect me and keep me safe on this death trap.

We accelerate and I let out a squeal. He doesn't go fast, moving with the traffic at a safe speed, which I'm grateful for. We drive down the main street by the beach, where people are walking and exercising on the sidewalks and others are on the beach. We pass my work, and he slows down, pulling off to the side to park.

I swing my leg over the bike and wait for him to get off to pass him the helmet.

"See," he says cheekily, "you didn't die."

It was only a short ride. My legs still feel unsteady. Much to my surprise, it wasn't as awful as I had imagined.

The small café has a checkered black-and-white floor and posters of Elvis Presley and Marilyn Monroe on the walls. We wait in line, and as we approach the counter, I notice the cashier pull her shoulders back, push her boobs out, bat her eyelashes, and give Axle a flirty grin.

"Hey, Axle," she coos.

He grins. "Morning." He turns to me. "What would you like?"

I peer up at the menu, which is on the wall. I open my mouth to ask what's good here, but as my eyes land on the server, she's looking at me with a pinched mouth. I peer back at Axle. "Pancakes, please."

He nods. "What flavor?"

"Buttermilk with honey."

He nods again, then peers back at the server. "Buttermilk pancakes with honey, and I'll have the big breakfast."

"Sure, and drinks?"

"Coffee and"—he peers at me—"a cappuccino please."

He steps closer to the register as she reads out the price, pays, and then leads me outside to a two-seater table, where we take a seat. I lift my bag to my lap and pull out my wallet. "Here," I say as I unzip it. "How much do I owe you?"

He waves me off. "Put it away. You'll never pay when you're with me."

I follow his instructions, then put my bag down. It's nice of him to pay.

"I want to get to know you," he says.

I clasp and unclasp my hands. "Why?"

He gives me a funny look. "What do you mean, why?"

"Out of all the girls on the website, why did you want to meet me?" I'm pretty sure he could have had any woman on the website, and it's clear from my brief interactions with him that women love him.

He gives me a thorough once-over. "Because you're fucking hot." Heat rises from my chest, up to my neck, and to my face. "And you seemed like a cool person to get to know."

I snort, then cough. *Real smooth* . . . "No one has ever called me cool."

"Who cares what anyone else says or thinks."

He has a point. It sucks that I care.

"My question is," he says, "why did you move here?"

"I wanted freedom, I guess you could say. I wanted a chance to experience what life has to offer outside of my hometown . . . It's my turn." So many questions run through my brain. I peer at his leather vest, which has a 1% and a War Brothers MC patch on it. "How did you become a member of a motorcycle club?"

"Most of my brothers, who are club members, were in the military. Me and Cash served together. When we got back from the war, we struggled to fit in."

It pains me to see the deep frown on his face as he pauses and looks away.

"We heard of a few veterans who were starting a motorcycle club, so we came to Crown Village to check it out. That's where we met Reaper, Bomber, and Viper. We all just clicked, so me and Cash never left. Then a few more members joined, and now there's seven of us."

A surge of shock courses through me. He's so much more than I thought.

He grins mischievously. "What do you do for fun?"

I pause, trying to find my words. I'm boring as hell.

"You know what fun is, right?"

My eyes narrow at the amusement in his voice. I lift my chin. "Yes."

He leans back lazily. "Then what do you do?"

"I read—"

He bursts out laughing.

"And I enjoy yoga," I add, making him laugh louder.

He slaps his thigh. "Aw, babe, you're so innocent. Don't you go to church too?"

I pout. "I used to. How do you know that?"

He leans over and touches my neck. I suck in a deep breath. I peek down as he pulls my necklace out and lies it on top of my shirt. My parents gave me the gold necklace with a cross pendant on my fourteenth birthday.

"Just a guess," he comments with a smirk, and then he leans back in his chair. That cheeky smile is addictive.

The server comes over and places our plates of food in front of us. My pancakes look delicious, with a swirl of cream on top and strawberries on the side. But as I inspect the pancakes further, I notice a pink tinge, which makes me think they're strawberry rather than buttermilk and honey.

"Here's my number," the server says seductively, "in case you lost it. You didn't call me back."

Axle's eyes narrow. "You can see I'm having breakfast with Elena. And anyway, if I didn't call you, it was on purpose." He waves her off.

The server and I flinch at the same time. I'm feeling secondhand embarrassment.

"Fucking rude bitch," he says under his breath as he watches her leave. Then he looks back at me. "What's wrong?" he asks, staring at my plate of food before looking back at me.

"Nothing."

"No, there's a problem with your food. I saw it all over your face before that chick started carrying on."

"I ordered buttermilk pancakes," I say softly. I hate making a fuss. "I think this might be strawberry."

He leans over and takes my plate, but I grasp the other side of it. "Don't worry, it's fine," I whisper, not wanting to make a scene.

His nose crinkles. "No, it's not okay."

His unwavering gaze makes me let go of the plate. He's not the type to give in. I shrink in my chair with my head bowed as he goes back inside the café. I sit up when I hear his heavy footsteps return.

"You weren't going to say anything, were you?" he asks. "You were just going to eat them, knowing it wasn't what you ordered."

I grudgingly nod. People pleaser . . . that's me.

He shakes his head. "Don't be shy. If there's a problem, say it. Don't let people walk over you."

I offer him a small smile, appreciating that he stuck up for me. I already know it's something I need to work on. Being constantly criticized by my mother has left its scars.

"You want some of my food while you're waiting?" he asks. His enormous plate of food includes ham, sausages, eggs, bacon, a hash brown, and toast.

"No, thank you."

He picks up a piece of the crispy bacon and takes a bite. "Good, I'm not one to share."

This man has no filter, but he's a giant goofball. "Are you really going to eat all that?" I ask in disbelief.

His smile answers my question. "You bet I am."

"Your profile said you're a mechanic. Where do you work?"

"I'm the road captain of the War Brothers MC and I service, fix, and modify our motorcycles. I'm not a qualified mechanic, though, so I just do it for our club."

"What's a road captain?"

"I plan our rides, ensure our safety, service our bikes. That type of thing."

I tilt my head. "And you get paid to do that?"

After taking a huge bite of egg on toast, he replies, "Sure do."

Wow . . . he's pretty lucky. "What do you mean, you're not a qualified mechanic?"

"Ah-ah-*ah*," he says, wagging his index finger from side to side. "My turn to ask a question."

A sliver of annoyance flows through me. I'm greedy for more information. He's intriguing. I've never known anyone like him.

"Why'd you talk to me? Am I just a one-night stand to brag to your friends about?"

"No!" I shriek, utterly insulted. "Mel created the profile."

He snorts. "It's okay. You don't have to lie. I know you think I'm sexy."

I open, close, then open my mouth. I'm lost for words, and I blush. He's very good looking with that square jaw, piercing eyes, manly beard, and permanent devilish grin, but I'm not telling him that. His head is already too big for his shoulders.

"It's true," I say.

He chuckles. "Whatever helps you sleep at night," he coos.

I laugh, but then I remember what he said. "And I do *not* have one-night stands."

He adds a cheeky wink. "I'm just teasing."

After a moment of silence, I ask. "What did you mean you're not a *qualified* mechanic?"

"I'm just as skilled," Axle says confidently. "I was never good at school. I think I'm dyslexic or whatever it's called, so I suck at anything that has to do with reading or writing." He pauses and looks away. "The only reason I learned about fixing bikes was because I stole parts from an old man up the road from our trailer who owned a mechanic shop, and I sold them. When I did it again, he caught me and said he wouldn't call the cops if I paid him off by helping him in the garage, so I did. After the cleaning jobs, he saw I was interested in the bikes he was fixing, so he taught me things, and after that I helped him every day. I loved it."

His bright smile warms my chest. "Do you still spend time with him?" I ask.

His face falls, and I'm immediately filled with regret for asking such personal questions, but I want to get to know him.

"No, he's been dead for a while now."

I'm floored by his honesty, but grateful he shared it with me, nonetheless. "Did your parents care that you spent all your time there?"

"God, you're just going straight for the jugular with these questions." He snorts. "I could have been dead and my parents wouldn't have cared. Too busy getting high in the trailer we called a home."

I lean over and lay my hand on his. "I'm so sorry to hear that," I say sincerely. My heart aches for him. Something flashes across his face before he masks it with a smile, though there's still vulnerability in his eyes.

"I'm okay, babe. It was a long time ago, and I wouldn't change it for the world, otherwise I would have never met Victor, the owner of the garage, or built a life in the MC."

He's an open book, and I'm really liking that about him. He speaks his mind, and it's refreshing. "Thank you for sharing." I mean it. He looks like a badass biker, but he's more than that. Behind the vest are many layers of who he is as a person. I'm captivated by him. Even though I shouldn't be getting involved with him, I crave to know more.

My pancakes arrive and I smile at the server, whose head is bowed. She promptly turns on her heel and goes back inside.

Axle lifts his cup to his mouth and drinks. I watch his Adam's apple bob up and down. I have no idea how that's attractive, but it is.

He leans back. "Let me guess, you were a good girl and, being the book nerd that you are, you did well at school."

I cringe. "Maybe . . ." He's exactly right.

Axle chuckles. "Oh yeah. You're pretty much the opposite of me in every way."

I gnaw on my lip, not sure whether it's a bad thing or not.

After I eat my pancakes, we chat briefly before we get up. He wraps an arm around my shoulders, pulling me to his side, where I smell his cologne mixed with the leather of his vest, and I suppress a moan. Even though I'm startled for a second, I smile up at him. My heart is hammering, but his playful grin disarms me. Surprisingly, I feel a level of ease I never imagined I would experience with him.

We get on his bike, and I smile during the short ride home. Once home, I get off the bike and hand him the helmet, he grabs my arm and pulls me in close. He groans. "I don't kiss women, but I'm fighting the urge to kiss you right now."

My eyes go to his lips, craving a taste. "Well, don't," I whisper. Kissing him is my first instinct. I want to be soaked in his sin.

His eyes widen, then darken. My heart beats heavily. He grasps my necklace, pulls me to him, and captures my lips in a firm kiss. Sheer desire fuels me and I press my lips against his. Hard.

Time freezes. I'm leaning against him and his bike. My hands slip around his neck, my mouth parting. His tongue slides in and meets mine, holding me hypnotized. I whimper into his mouth. His arm tightens around me as my body heats up. With each movement of his tongue against mine, a rush of lust courses through my body, traveling from my veins to my groin. His kiss is demanding and authoritative. I'm at his mercy.

The long, lingering kiss makes my lips crave his as soon as he pulls away. I'm left panting, my head spinning.

His eyes are dark as his thumb caresses my bottom lip. "Looks like an angel, kisses like a demon."

My eyes latch onto his lips again. Axle is trouble, but I can't stop the way my body reacts to him.

I step backward and watch as he revs his engine, pulls out, and does a burnout, his tires leaving black skid marks. My eyes narrow. He shouldn't put himself in danger like that.

I touch my now-plump lips. There's cheering and clapping behind me. I turn my gaze toward the house and notice my roommates. I walk over to them.

"You never mentioned that you know Axle! That's so exciting!" Lucy exclaims, bouncing enthusiastically beside me.

I give her a small smile.

"All those motorcycle club men are hot," Cindy chimes in.

"So where did you meet him?" Jasmine asks, not sharing her friend's enthusiasm.

"Uh, the restaurant." I don't want them to know it was on a dating app.

I like the attention Axle is giving me. Getting attention is new to me, and while he's talking to me, I don't want to share him, regardless of whether they have boyfriends or not.

"Cameron would have hated that," Lia says with a laugh.

I think back and flinch. "Yes, he did. I'm going to go upstairs and relax before I start my shift."

I dart up the stairs, close my bedroom door, and lie on my bed, confused. Axle's a conundrum. A small part of me is still wary of him, but a much bigger part of me wants to learn more about him. He's friendly and warm. There's more to him than what a motorcycle club vest says. That he told me about parts of his life in such a vulnerable way has only increased my curiosity.

I don't know what came over me, but I wanted to kiss him, and as soon as our lips touched, I couldn't stop myself. I was drenched in his scent, his touch, his lips. A wave of euphoria unlike anything I had felt before surged through me. It was as if every cell in my body was buzzing, a sensation so intense that it left me breathless.

I wonder what he meant by not kissing women. He doesn't seem like one to lie, so I gather it's true, but it has me questioning why he kissed *me* then.

I wish I was close to my sister Ava again so that I can talk to her about it. She got married and I guess she got busy. She doesn't reply much anymore. I miss her so much, especially at times like this. While I don't generally hate people, I'm angry at her husband for taking her away from me.

AT WORK I'M JUST GOING THROUGH THE MOTIONS. MY MIND IS elsewhere. I'm quiet when Mel asks about the date, even though she's persistent and asks me loads of questions. I keep it to a bare minimum and don't dare say anything about the kiss.

After my shift, I get into my car and pull my phone out of my bag. There's a message from Axle.

Axle

> Hey babe, I enjoyed spending the morning with you. Your kiss was the sweetest thing I've ever tasted. When can I see you again?

I gasp, panicking. What if I gave him the wrong idea? I hastily respond.

> I'm not having sex with you.

> Hahaha chill, babe. I want to spend time with you again.

I gaze up and peer at the ocean. I wanted to experience life . . . It's only another date. I refuse to look back and regret not taking a chance. It's not often I'm noticed by a good-looking man like him.

I take a deep breath and type.

> Okay, I'll see you after work. Pick me up from my house.

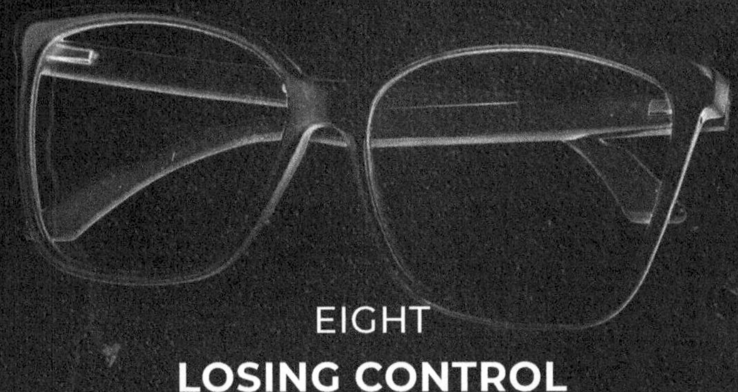

EIGHT

LOSING CONTROL

Elena

MY ROOMMATES WERE QUIET LAST NIGHT, BUT AS I CREEP DOWN the stairs, I hear them. Of all the days I was hoping to sneak out of the house without seeing anyone, they just happen to all be awake. The girls are at the kitchen counter, Jasmine with a coffee and Lucy and Cindy eating cereal out of bowls.

As I walk in further, I spot Jeremy. "Here she is," he says, and all eyes are on me. I swallow hard and smile.

As I walk to the coffee machine, Jeremy steps over toward me. "Axle from the motorcycle club, hey? I heard the War Brothers Motorcycle Club parties are epic. You'll have to invite us when you go."

"Oh yes," Cindy chimes in.

"Woah!" I say and lift my hand. "I've only just met Axle." Would I like to get to know him more? Possibly.

"Lucy said you were kissing him," Jasmine says, pouting.

My eyes flick straight to Lucy, but she looks away, avoiding eye contact.

"I'm just saying, we're all friends, so don't forget about us," Jeremy says.

"I can't believe you went on a date with him. Those bikers don't date. Are you seeing him again?" asks Jasmine.

I'm not a liar, but a part of me wants to lie to them. "I'm seeing him today, after work." Lucy and Cindy squeal in unison, making me flinch.

"I've never known any of them to go on dates. They only have sex," says Jasmine matter-of-factly. Lucy swats her arm.

The coffee machine beeps, signaling that my coffee is ready, but the conversation has put me off, so I grab the mug and empty the drink down the sink. I'm not sure whether Jasmine was suggesting that I was lying or that I was sleeping with him, so I say, "Well, I told Axle I'm not having sex with him, and he still wants to see me."

Lucy shakes her head. "Don't worry about Jasmine. She's jealous. I've heard Axle's a wild one, but have fun, and I want to hear all about it when you get back from your date."

Cindy sighs. "He's got heartbreak written all over him."

"If you think he wants anything more than a quick fuck, you're sorely mistaken."

I step back, puzzled by Jasmine's snappishness.

"Just let her have her fun," Lucy pipes up.

Jasmine rolls her eyes. "You're heading for disaster. Don't say I didn't warn you."

I give them a forced smile and hurry out. My breaths are shaky as I get in my car and pull the door closed. They've made me doubt myself, but it still doesn't make sense. Why would Axle waste his time when I've said I won't sleep with him if that's all he wants? He evidently has no issues getting women.

After my short drive to work, I walk into the restaurant to see Mel and Cameron at the counter. When they look up at me, Mel's eyes narrow and Cameron shakes his head. My stomach drops. What have I done wrong? I frantically think back to the last shift. I don't recall making any mistakes.

Despite the leisurely pace with which I approach them, my heart races. I need this job. I'll just apologize and tell Cameron that whatever I've done wrong, it won't happen again.

"You're a liar," Mel says bitterly.

I sharply inhale. "What did I lie about?"

"You said your date was uneventful. I didn't realize hooking up outside your house with Axle was uneventful for you. If he's so boring, I'll have him."

That's what they're annoyed about. I was stressed out, thinking I had done something wrong at work. I exhale slowly. She's testing me, even though I hate conflict. If she likes Axle so much, I can't understand why she told me to talk to him.

"I didn't feel it was necessary to share every detail about the date."

"I'm surprised you'd associate yourself with the likes of him." Disgust drips from Cameron's every word. "He's a criminal . . . the whole MC is bad news."

Mel scoffs. "You don't know that. What do they do to make them criminals?"

Cameron crosses his arms in front of him. "Everyone knows they are."

Mel gives him a pointed look. "You can't even answer the question. You don't know what the MC does."

When Cameron turns to me, his gaze softens. "I'm worried about you. I don't know why you'd put yourself in danger like that."

Mel puts her arm around my shoulders and walks me away from Cameron. "Just ignore Cameron. He's jealous that the MC members get more ass than him. If I thought Axle was dangerous, I'd tell you. It surprised me that you're going on dates with him because I didn't think he dated." I experience a slight sense of relief until she says, "The good girl falling for the bad boy. God help you!"

"I'm not falling for him."

She raises a brow. "Are you planning to see him again?"

I hesitate before I answer. "After work."

A slow smile curves across her lips. "You wouldn't see him again if you weren't interested."

Back home after my shift, I sift through my wardrobe with a growing sense of dread. I have no idea what to wear. He'll be here any minute. My hands tremble slightly as I pull on my favorite light-blue jeans and a pale pink T-shirt.

I've straightened my long blond hair, and I'm wearing lip balm and light makeup. With each step down the stairs, my nervousness intensifies. My hands feel clammy. He's probably used to being with confident, beautiful women, and I'm nothing like that. I peer down at what I'm wearing and wince. I hesitate and think about changing, but then I hear the familiar rumble of a motorcycle. This will have to do.

I bolt down the last few steps and outside, grateful that all my roommates are at college. As I walk out the door, Axle's pulling his helmet off. I quicken my pace, and his eyes meet mine. He smiles, making me smile right back. Excitement and nerves collide within me while I head toward his bike. I should take others' opinions lightly and decide for myself about him.

With his wicked trademark smile, he says, "Ready to go for a ride?"

"Sure," I answer as I glance down at his bike, remembering how fun the last ride was. But then I whack him.

He rubs his arm, exaggerating the pain. "What was that for?"

"The burnout you did. Don't do it—it's dangerous. You could have been hurt."

He stares at me a while before he says, "I've been doing tricks on bikes my whole life. I know what I'm doing."

I shake my head, then jut out my chin. "It's reckless and I don't like it."

He grants me a genuine smile. "I won't do it around you. How's that?"

"I'd prefer you not do it at all." Why risk the chance of getting hurt?

"Hmmm . . . bossy. I like it." He slips the helmet over my head and fastens the straps under my chin, then takes a step back as his eyes caress every inch of my body. "You're sexy as fuck, babe."

"Thank you," I murmur, my voice barely above a whisper. I felt underdressed before, but the hunger in his eyes makes me feel truly seen for the first time and strangely validated. "You look good too," falls from my mouth. *I'm so lame.*

He chuckles. "Yeah, I do." He's oh so modest.

I climb onto the bike and shuffle closer to him. I lace my arms wrap around his torso. His body feels lean and athletic. It stirs a curiosity in me about what he might look like shirtless, a thought that starts a small thrill fluttering in my stomach. The sensation is both exciting and frightening, and I'm acutely aware of the danger he represents—in more ways than one.

"Hold on tight," Axle says over the rumble of the bike. He pulls the motorcycle out onto the road.

The gust of air on my face and the road rushing beneath me have me smiling widely. With my cheek pressed against his back, I peer out as we pass by the beach and ride further along to the lake, where he parks in the closest parking spot.

When I get off the bike, my smile comes naturally. "That's so much fun!"

After he gets off the bike, I pass him the helmet, and he hangs it over one handlebar. "You're easy to please . . . No need to thank me."

He pulls me into him, his arm around my shoulders, and we walk across the grass to the sand. As we stroll along, I gaze up at him. "Are you trying to woo me, sweep me off my feet with a walk along the water?" I tease.

His lip twitches. "Is it working?"

I press my lips together, not wanting to sound too eager. Since I've met him, it's been a whirlwind of surprises. Walking along the lake was not what I expected we would be doing. Everyone was so wrong about him.

"I'll take that as a yes," he says, grinning smugly.

I don't argue the point. "What made you choose the lake?" I ask instead.

"I prefer not to be surrounded by civilians." He chuckles as he peers down at the sand. "Dating is new to me, so I didn't know where else to go."

"Next time, it would be great to just hang out at home. Watch a few movies or something."

"Next time?" he smirks. "Netflix and chill," he adds in an overly sexual voice. He chuckles. That sounds like so much more than just watching Netflix.

"Well, yes . . . just hanging out watching TV."

He grabs his chest like he's in pain. "Don't sound too enthusiastic. You're breaking my big biker heart," he teases.

I've come to learn it's just him. Everything is highly amusing, and he's got no filter. He says it in a way that's not sleazy, but everything's a joke to him. He's cheeky and quick-witted.

I playfully elbow him. "I'll hang out with you . . . but I'm not having sex with you," I say with my chin high in the air as I smother a smile.

"You're missing out," he quips. "I'll fucking ruin you for every other man."

My body heats and my cheeks burn. I rub my forehead. I need to snap out of it. I like the attention, but what sane, straight woman wouldn't like the attention of a sexy, fun biker with a killer smile?

"Where do you live?" I ask.

"At the clubhouse with the rest of my War Brothers MC brothers."

"Do you guys have parties there?" I ask, since everyone keeps talking about them.

His smile kicks up. "Yeah, we do."

I wonder what his friends are like. If they are anything like him, I think I'll like them too. "Will I get to meet your friends?"

He stops walking, so I pause. He's giving me a strange look. "Let me get this straight. You want to meet my friends . . . the bikers?"

I'm curious, but also a little scared. "I'm interested in learning more about you." He seems close to his friends.

He laughs and pulls me in tighter. "You're always surprising me."

That goes both ways. I remember all of them riding down the street, dressed up in black and leather, on their motorcycles. I frown. "What are they like? Will they hurt me?"

"What? Hell no. We don't hurt women."

"Do you all have orgies? I know you do illegal stuff, but how illegal? Do you kill people?" The word vomit is unstoppable.

He laughs. "Some people have sex with more than one person at once."

So that's a yes.

"And no, we just don't go around killing people." He didn't say he hadn't, though. "I can't tell you about what we do. It's club business. Being in our motorcycle club means we don't answer to anybody but ourselves when it comes to our brothers and our club."

"I've never experienced having friends who are like family. It must feel great to belong somewhere."

He picks me up, wraps my legs around his hips, and puts his hands on my ass. I squeal, then laugh in surprise.

"I think you're belonging somewhere right about now." His voice is raspy and seductive, but his eyes remain playful.

Stupidity and lust drive my arms around his neck, my hands snaking to the back of his head, into his hair, while I lean in and touch my lips to his. It starts off slow, but in true Axle fashion, it takes no time to become heated. My skin burns as our tongues duel and the passion intensifies. He squeezes my ass. I softly tug his hair, enticing a groan from his lips.

A phone rings faintly in the background, making him pause. "Fuck," he mumbles. He gently places me on my feet and brings his phone to his ear.

"Yeah," he answers. "Now?" He growls. "*Fine.* I'm on my way." He peers back at me. "Sorry, babe. I've got church."

I can't help but laugh. "You go to church? Really?"

"Not that type of church. It's where we hold club meetings."

My shoulders drop. Our date has been cut short. "Oh, okay."

He cups my jaw and searches my eyes. "Are you sure you want to meet my friends?"

Axle isn't as bad as people say. I'm sure his friends are the same, but I'd be silly not to feel some apprehension. I mutter, "Sure," trying to mask my uncertainty.

"You're going to see shit you're not going to like, and the

men cuss like me." He's giving me an out, but I still want to go.

"You and your friends can cuss in front of me. I'm not a saint."

He flashes me a sexy smile. "I know that. Take tomorrow's lunch shift off, and I'll bring you to the clubhouse then."

I bite my lip. As much as I'd like to, I can't lose this job. "I can't. I'm working."

His brows furrow. "The night shift too?" he asks.

I nod. "I'm new. I need to make a good impression."

"Oh, you've made an impression alright," he says, sarcasm lacing his voice.

"What's that supposed to mean?" I ask defensively.

"I. Told. You. Your boss wants to bang you. The guy's a creep and a pussy. Don't trust him."

I still. Axle's tone is mainly playful, but there's an edge to it I haven't heard before. I have Cameron warning me about Axle, and Axle warning me about Cameron, which is a little confusing. But I want to be independent . . . That means I get to choose who I'm friends with based on my own opinions and nobody else's.

"The atmosphere is different later in the night at the clubhouse. Don't yell at me when you hate it."

I scoff. "I won't yell at you."

I get on the motorcycle, and we ride back to mine. Every minute, disappointment festers. I yearn to get to know him. The short dates haven't been enough, and I still have so many questions. It's been eye-opening getting to know someone so different from me. We might be opposites, but we get along like I've known him for years.

After I get off his bike, I remove the helmet and pass it to him.

"I'll see you tomorrow night," he says softly.

I lean in to kiss him, but he pulls back. One of his hands is twitching by his side. "I only have so much self-control. I want to stay with you, but I really need to get back to the clubhouse, and the way *you* kiss . . ." He shakes his head. "Let's just say, your halo doesn't fool me."

I'm smiling a big, cheesy smile right back at him.

NINE
MEETING THE MC

Elena

I STARE DOWN AT THE DRESS I'M WEARING THAT I BOUGHT during my lunch break. It's a far cry from what I usually wear, with spaghetti straps and a hem that falls above my knees. It's no minidress but look out—I'm living life on the edge. I chuckle to myself.

I'm not sure if a dress is appropriate to wear. In my determination to look good for Axle, I didn't consider that a dress may not be practical on the back of a bike. But I can't ask anyone now, and anyway, I want to look and feel sexy. I'm sure he's used to glamorous women. I can't remember a time when I ever felt sexy. Henry made me feel pretty, but never sexy. I slip my sandals on, then stand up straight.

"Oh crap! Oh crap!" I grasp my racing heart. What if Axle wants me to stay the night? I didn't ask about my ride home. I pace. I didn't think this through. The rumble of a motorcycle makes me shriek in panic. I grab a bag and throw in some pajamas. I rush out to the bathroom and grab my toothbrush.

My breathing is out of control as I walk downstairs. Everyone's out, so the house is quiet. I open the front door to go outside. I can do this. I can do this . . . *No, I can't do this.* I retreat and start closing the front door.

"Hold up," Axle calls out, pulling the door open wide. "First"—his eyes ravish my body, making me blush—"you look fucking hot, babe. Second, you're not going anywhere. You committed to meeting my friends, so get your sexy self on my bike." He reaches over and takes my hand in his. "I'd never let anyone hurt you." He pulls me in for a brief hug.

I embrace his warmth and feel a sliver of relief. I believe him. He places a gentle kiss on my forehead, making me swoon and smile up at him. My stomach churns with mixed emotions.

When he sees the bag on my shoulder, he asks, with a wicked glint in his eyes, "Staying the night, are you?"

"I didn't know," I stutter out. "We didn't talk about when or how I was getting home."

He chuckles. "It's okay—I get it. You're keen to see me naked."

I scoff and choke at the same time. "That thought never came to my mind. I told you I'm not having sex with you."

He points to the corner of my mouth. "You're drooling just at the thought of it."

I'm tongue-tied before I can even contemplate a response. He lifts his shirt, displaying his fit body. My mouth drops open at the display of muscles. He pulls my hand to the top of his abs and slowly drags it down his torso. His skin is warm and taut. I yank my hand back before it reaches the top of his jeans. It felt so good, but I glare at him while I scold myself. Before I can utter a word, he tips his chin and says, "You loved it," and then kisses the air.

I blow out a breath, puffing out my cheeks. I take a slow step outside, trying to gather my wits about me. I turn and lock the door before we walk to his bike. He's out of control, but I always end up smiling or laughing at him. He's not the typical broody, intimidating biker. With his playful and flirty nature, it's no surprise he's popular with the ladies.

"Excited for your first club party, babe?"

"Hmm . . . party?" I ask, hoping I misheard him.

"It's just a quiet one, chill out . . . breathe . . ."

My heart is in my throat. I feel a storm of emotions swirling inside me. Am I anxious about the party or irritated by his condescending tone? Maybe it's both. My hands tremble slightly, and I catch myself clenching my jaw, trying to mask the frustration that's creeping onto my face. All I wanted to do was casually meet his friends, not be surrounded by drunk people. I don't do parties . . . *ever*.

After he gets on his bike, I stay standing. I look at him, his bike, and then the ground. "You're going to keep me safe, aren't you?"

"I've got you," he says soothingly. "I'll be with you the whole night. My friends are good people. You'll see."

I decide to have an exit plan just in case. "I'm only going if I drive my car."

He shrugs. "All good. You can follow me."

I appreciate that he didn't argue the point. He turns the ignition on and the bike roars to life. While I walk toward my car, he calls out, "I knew you wanted to see me naked."

I chuckle as I walk to the car. He's impossible.

As we drive through town, it's mostly quiet. Past the residential area and the shops, he speeds up before veering off on a dirt road. They must live on an acreage. He slows when we reach a huge two-story farmhouse. He leads me through the gate and drives off to the side and into an open shed. When he turns the bike off, there's loud music coming from the house.

There's a light on in the shed, so I can see a line of motor-cycles, a big black truck, and a van. I remain in my car just outside the doors. "Where do I park?" I ask as he walks toward me.

"Park it in the shed next to the van."

I give him a cautious glance. *Park* . . . I cringe. Not that there are any lines, but still. "My car won't fit in there."

He walks around the car and opens my door. "Move over."

I take my seat belt off and shuffle over to the passenger seat. When he gets in, I fight back a laugh because he's doing me a favor. He has to just about fold himself in half to fit in my small car and is nearly kissing the dashboard.

He adjusts the seat, closes the door, and shoots me a look that says not to say a word. I press my lips together to hold back my laughter. I relax in my seat as he smoothly maneuvers the car into the parking spot. And there's something sexy about a man who's a confident driver.

"Trust you to have the world's smallest car . . . and what's this crap?" He gestures toward the speakers.

I huff. "It is *not* crap. It's Cardi B."

He turns the car off. "It's crap. You listening to rap is funny as hell, though."

Outside the shed, he puts an arm around my shoulders, pulling me to his side, and ushers me toward the house. My pulse skyrockets, and I'm seriously questioning my life choices.

"Tell me if you're going to faint and I'll catch you."

I tsk. He laughs.

"I'm not going to faint." I don't think I am . . . Well, I hope not.

"I'm just teasing you," he replies with the devilish grin he wears so well.

I peer up at the farmhouse. I'm walking into the lion's den. I lower my head as we walk through the front door. He leads me through a hallway that opens into an open-plan space. I pause, unsure of where to direct my gaze. My heart beats in sync with the heavy beat of the music.

My eyes bounce from one man to another. These guys are not what I'm used to . . . They're all tall, masculine men wearing similar clothes: jeans, a shirt, and the club vest. I'm not used to this much testosterone. Two intimidating men are playing pool. Further behind them, at the bar, sits a man with black hair, his back to us. A few people are playing darts.

One wall is adorned with a large black flag that bears the same logo that's on the club vests: a skull set over two crossed guns, with "War Brothers MC" written above it. At the rear of the room, a literal motorcycle is recessed in the wall . . . they really love their motorcycles. My eyes wander further. I squint. Is that . . .? I squeal and turn on my heel so damn fast.

Axle gently holds my face and raises my head to make eye contact. "What's wrong?"

I blush furiously. "Two people are having sex on the couch." I never imagined I'd say this, but here I am.

"Fuuuck." He looks over to them. "I'll be right back."

"Viper, put your dick back into your pants," he yells over the music.

I wince. I've never wished to fade into the background as much as I do at this moment. The music quietens, and I hear the hum of conversation.

Axle is by my side again. "All good now—he's got his pants on," he says casually, as if having sex in public is normal.

We turn around to face his friends. I keep my eyes closed for a moment before chancing a look.

"I told them to calm it down a bit, but"—he looks up, his

eyes fixed on his friend—"it looks like Viper didn't hear me," he says loudly.

"Sorry, man," his friend calls out. The apology sounds half-hearted, more teasing than sincere. I can't even look at his friend Viper now.

Axle drags me over to his friends at the pool table. They both pause and glance between us. Since my body is frozen, all I can manage is a stupid stare. I thought Axle was tall, but the man closest to me is enormous—I'm shorter than his shoulders. "This is Reaper, our president. We call him Reaper or Pres."

Reaper tips his head to me in greeting. "You sure you know what you're getting yourself into with him?" he asks in a deep, rough voice, tilting his head in Axle's direction.

My gaze shifts from Axle to Reaper.

Axle just laughs. "Oh, Pres has got jokes." But Reaper's not laughing.

I kind of wished I'd stayed home. Meeting Axle's friends is a car crash of embarrassment.

The other man has made his way to us. He's good looking, with dark features. His warm smile puts me at ease somewhat. "My name's Cash."

I smile back. "Oh . . . you're Axle's friend he went to the military with. My name's Elena," I say enthusiastically as I put my hand out. *I put my freaking hand out to shake a biker's hand.* I could hit my forehead right about now. Cash shakes my hand and I'm grateful he didn't embarrass me, but I don't miss the odd look and raised brow he gives Axle.

"I bet he's keeping you on your toes," Cash says.

"What does that mean?" Axle asks, the accusation clear in his tone.

"That he is," I answer Cash, and he chuckles.

Axle tugs me to the back of the room. "Cash is our treasurer. He's really smart. Manages all our stuff and does whatever a finance person does."

"What's with all the unusual names?" I ask. I watch the man by himself at the bar finish his drink, slam the glass on the counter, and leave. He does not seem happy.

Axle snorts. "Everyone calls each other by their road name, not by their actual name."

I pause. "So your real name's not Axle?"

He chuckles. "That's right."

I'm about to ask what it is, but we reach the dart players. A man wearing a cap that's been turned backward throws a dart and nearly hits the bullseye. "Hell yeah," he chants. When he sees us, he gives us a cheery smile. "Hey, I'm Twitch."

Another player, an attractive woman with long, dark hair, puts an arm around his waist. She gives me a quick up and down glance. "I'm Mercedez."

"Twitch is our security and IT expert," Axle says.

Before I can reply, a heavily tattooed man makes his way over to us. He has a mohawk and an eerie aura that makes me take a step back. I gasp when I see the shine of a blade and watch in horror as he throws his knife at the dartboard, hitting the bullseye.

"And that's Demon, our enforcer," Axle says.

I don't know what that means, and I'm pretty sure I don't want to find out.

Twitch scowls at Demon. "You're a cheat!"

Demon smirks and walks away.

I'm at a loss for words as I stare wide-eyed at the dartboard. Who in their right mind throws a knife near people? I plan to keep all my limbs, so I'm staying far away from him.

"My girl here is mute," says Axle, amused.

I playfully shove him. "I am not." I turn to Twitch and

Mercedez, say, "Hi," and give them an awkward wave and a tight smile. Why am I incapable of being normal?

Two women off to the side are giving me the death stare. One, her hair in a bob, is dressed classier than her red-haired companion, who is wearing similar clothing—or a lack of clothing—as the other women. I lean closer to Axle. "Who are they?" I ask.

He turns his head, then his eyes narrow. His arm around my shoulder tightens. "They're no one . . . Come on, let's go get you a drink." He pauses. "You do drink, right, or are you all work and no play?"

"Just one drink," I mutter. I peer back to see both women still glaring at me, looks of disgust on their faces. I exhale noisily. I have no desire to get involved in any drama. Do they not like me or is it because I came here with Axle?

Axle leads me deeper into the house, to the back, where there's a large kitchen. He pulls open the fridge door, leans in, and grabs two small bottles, one with a brightly colored label. He takes the lid off one and hands it to me. The drink is purple. I take a mouthful to ease my nerves.

"See?" Axle's smile is goofy. "I told you it would be fine meeting my friends."

"How was that fine?" Public sex, knife throwing . . . not to mention my incessant need to embarrass myself. "This is a quiet night?" What would a big party be then?

The couple that was shamelessly having sex walk in. They are smiling as they walk toward me. No embarrassment whatsoever. I'm blushing enough for the two of them.

"This is Viper, our vice president," Axle points out.

Viper is handsome and has a beard. He wears the same devilish grin Axle wears. The girl is short and petite like me, sporting the same long blond hair. I thought I was showing a lot of skin in my new dress, but she's wearing short shorts that are undone at the front and a bikini top that barely covers her nipples.

"It's good to meet you. I've heard *all* about you," Viper says, his voice heavy with inuendo. His eyes slowly drift over me.

The woman steps closer to me with a bright smile. "I'm Candy. You've been the topic of conversation around here."

I peer at Axle. He's waving his fingers in front of his throat, gesturing for her to stop talking. That's rude of him. I bring the bottle to my lips and take another gulp to hide my discomfort. I hate being the topic of conversation.

"You alright?" Viper asks me.

I stiffen, surprised at how observant he is. "Yes, I'm just getting a little tired." Minor lie for the greater good. Being with them . . . it's overwhelming.

Axle takes my drink and sets it on the kitchen counter. "Come on, let's go upstairs."

Viper laughs. "You're going to bed now? The party hasn't even started yet."

In that case, I'm glad we're leaving.

"Whatever my girl wants, she gets."

Axle is smiling down at me with warm eyes, and I melt into a puddle by his feet.

"Your girl . . ." Viper's voice is loud with disbelief. "So you're together?"

"No," I reply. I like Axle, but I just got out of a relationship and I don't know if Axle could commit.

Axle clicks his tongue. "Not yet," he says, then gives me a wink.

Axle's charm . . . his humor . . . his looks . . . deadly combination. He's trouble with a capital *T*. It both scares and excites me.

As we pass by the couple, Candy says, "Good night."

I pick up on Viper muttering something about money as

we walk by. Axle kisses my temple, looks over his shoulder, and says, "Yeah, you will."

As we leave the kitchen by the opposite door, we pass by a wall decorated with mug shots. I try to look at them, but Axle pulls me closer, encouraging me to walk faster. But then I spot Axle's photo. Even in the picture there's a smugness in his eyes and the slight tilt of his lips.

"Why is your mug shot on the wall? What did you do?"

He lowers his head. "Nothing. Stress less, babe. Keep walking."

As we make our way up the staircase, I gaze down at everyone. Being here is like being in another universe, though I'm not sure what I expected. I spot the motorcycle recessed into the wall again. I shift my eyes to Axle. "Why do you have a motorcycle inside the clubhouse?" It makes no sense.

His shoulders tense and he falls silent. When we reach the top of the stairs, he says, "It was Victor's."

The solemnity of his reply startles me. In a rare moment of vulnerability, his face softens and a frown tugs at his lips. Guilt hits me.

We walk to the end of a hall that's lined with bedroom doors, most of them closed. As he opens one, I say, "I'm sorry. I didn't mean to pry."

He ushers me into the room, closes the door, and gives me a smile that doesn't reach his eyes. "No need to say sorry."

His answer doesn't ease my guilt. He might be all smiles, but when it comes to losing his father figure, he can't mask the hurt in his eyes.

I look around. His room has a navy-blue feature wall. Against it stands his black bed frame, and his bed is made with black bedding. Another War Brothers MC flag hangs on the wall opposite the bed.

Axle is observing me closely. He slips off his leather vest and sets it down on the cabinet below the TV.

My breathing is erratic as he walks toward me. "I'm not having sex with you," I say again, not quite sure who I'm trying to convince at this point.

He laughs. "I know," he says, then grabs his chest as if someone shot him. "No need to keep reminding me, you're going to hurt my feelings."

I scoff. "I highly doubt that."

He fights a smile and sits down. He pulls off his boots, then shuffles over and lies down on his side. I admire his face. That square jaw . . . those full lips. It's criminal how attractive he is.

He pats the bed beside him. I give him a cautious stare.

"I'm not going to have sex with you," he says, his grin mischievous as he throws my words back at me in the same tone I use. "Unless you want me to," he purrs.

I struggle to hide my smile, but I stay standing. His bed looks daunting . . . lying down . . . next to him. After that kiss we shared, I question my self-control. He's watching me, but he's not forcing the issue, so I take a deep breath, though my heart is pounding, and slowly sit, then lie beside him. My breath catches in my throat when he shuffles over, closing the space between us. A blend of anticipation and nervousness ripples through me.

"You're too trusting."

I become rigid and try to sit up, but he pulls me back down.

"You came back to the clubhouse with me . . . you're in my bedroom. I wouldn't do anything if you didn't want to, but if I was someone different, you could have put yourself in a bad situation."

I turn away and stare at the wall. Am I so desperate for a connection with someone that I'd trust so blindly?

Axle grasps my chin and turns my face toward his until our eyes meet. "What are you thinking about?"

"Everything is new to me . . ." I never had the chance to make poor choices. I surrounded myself with like-minded friends and a like-minded boyfriend. We were the quiet, studious group that did well at school and kept to ourselves. "I've never had reason not to trust someone."

Something flashes across his face, then his brow furrows. "Promise me you'll be more careful." He's serious.

"So I should be more careful around you?"

His lip lifts. "Around everyone." His gaze quickly shifts to my lips, then back to my eyes. "But especially around me," he says before he leans down and presses a soft kiss to my shoulder, muting the voices inside my head. He plants a trail of kisses from my collarbone up my neck. A moan slips from my mouth as shivers rack my body.

His lips meet mine, and I'm helpless under his voodoo. I can't fight my attraction to him. My body flares to life, every part of me awakening. He slides his tongue into my mouth, shooting searing need through my body.

He pulls back an inch. "I'm obsessed with the way you taste," he growls, then his mouth is on mine again.

I lift my hand and gently run my fingers through his hair. He leans closer, pressing his weight against me, and an overwhelming need fills my mind. Bliss blankets me, while a deep longing pulses within. Our tongues dance together, and his grip on my hip becomes more insistent, pulling me closer.

He groans and eases back, dragging his teeth over my bottom lip. It's new to me, but the seductive way he did it . . . I liked it. I'm watching as his head falls back.

We both gasp for oxygen.

"Fuuuck. You can't kiss me like that," he murmurs, though his gaze lingers on my lips, betraying his words. He leans forward slightly, caught between resistance and desire.

I touch my tingling lips. The warmth of his kiss lingers, leaving behind a sensation of longing. I've never felt such desire for anyone . . . And I've never been kissed so passionately.

His eyes search mine, then his face softens. "I'm poison. You're going to regret meeting me."

Maybe . . . maybe not. "I'll make up my own mind." He never forced me into anything against my will. I wanted—no, I craved—his lips on mine. "I've enjoyed getting to know you." He's so different.

He lets out a sigh, leans down, and pulls the blanket up over us. "Turn around," he says, his voice still rough.

I roll over and he lies back down, pressing his body against mine. His chest is against my back, his arm encircling my body, cradling me against him. Warm and content, I smile. I shouldn't feel safe, but I do. I should be running away from him with what everyone else is saying, but I can't. I promised myself I'd make up my own mind about everyone I meet. In the short time I've known him, he's evoked emotions in me that I've never experienced before, which only compels me to spend more time with him.

The music from downstairs gets louder. I feel the vibrations from the bass. The voices have risen too. Maybe more people have arrived. My mind goes back to the motorcycle. "Can I ask you a question?"

"Sure, babe."

"Why is Victor's motorcycle inside?"

He's silent. I wait patiently.

"It's rare. Victor built it himself. I've never been able to bring myself to ride it—it's too important to me. So I asked the club if it could remain in the clubhouse, where it would be close by and I could always keep an eye on it."

He may wear a joker mask, but there's a loving man behind it. He isn't this horrible criminal and player everyone labels him as.

"What's your real name?" I ask.

"Jake."

"Jake," I say, tasting his name on my tongue. "Tell me more about yourself."

"Eh . . . what do you want to know?"

I pause. "Anything . . . Why did you steal parts from Victor, and what made you stick around and not go back to what you were doing before he caught you?"

"No one ever cared enough to teach me something. He helped me find something I was good at, and he looked after me."

Oh, my aching heart.

"I stole from him because I needed the money to eat and to help my parents pay the bills, but if I hadn't stolen from Victor, God knows where I would have ended up."

My parents may be unbearable, but I always had a roof over my head, clean clothes, and all the basic necessities. "What do you mean by not knowing where you may have ended up?"

"I was a menace to society." He chuckles. "I broke into people's houses and stole things. When the police found me with the stolen goods, I hopped on my motorbike and they had to chase me around in their vehicle. I loved the chase. To see how long it took them to get me. It happened a few times. I'd go to juvie, then get let back out."

Well, I see nothing has changed apart from the stealing. "And then you went into the military and met Cash?"

"I was angry when Victor died and hated the world, so yeah, I went into the military. Cash was my lifeline and just like me. We weren't in the military for long, though. We went overseas, served, and did our time, and that was enough for us. I think we're lucky that we left when we did. I see some of the others struggle with what they saw and experienced . . . especially Reaper. That shit haunts him."

Tears prick my eyes. "That's horrible."

"Awww, babe." He places a soft kiss on my shoulder that warms my heart. "Don't get upset. Life happens. Every club member has a shitty life story, but that's also what brought us together. Family is who you choose it to be." He hugs me tighter. "Now get some sleep."

"Bossy," I mutter.

"Damn straight. Night, babe."

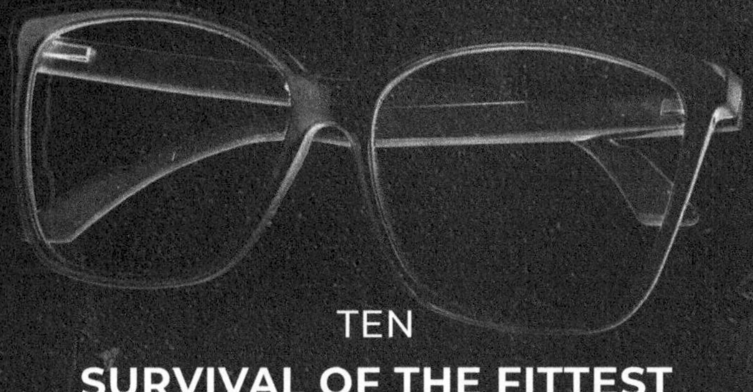

TEN
SURVIVAL OF THE FITTEST

Elena

My eyes flutter open to sunlight filtering through the curtains. The music from downstairs has turned into a quiet hum. My thoughts drift back to last night. I survived meeting his friends . . . barely. It's a different lifestyle here. I've never witnessed people having sex in public.

I need to go to the bathroom. I shuffle out of Axle's hold and peer back at him. He reaches for me, but then he drifts back off to sleep. He looks so peaceful. I don't want to wake him.

I crack open the door. I don't see anyone, so I step outside. Heavy footsteps approach. Viper comes jogging up, drenched in sweat and with his shirt tucked into the waistband of his shorts. He gives me a head tilt. "Mornin'."

"Good morning," I say with a smile. "Can you please tell me where the bathroom is?"

He points down the hallway. "The door right at the end."

"Thank you." I tread softly, trying not to wake anyone.

After going to the bathroom and washing my hands, I stare at my reflection in the mirror. The responsible version of me says I shouldn't have stayed overnight. The new, you-only-live-once version says screw it.

I cautiously open the door and creep back into Axle's room. He hasn't moved and is still fast asleep. I walk over to my bag and rummage through it, searching for my anxiety medication. I can't take my tablets without water, but the kitchen is downstairs. I peer back at Axle and wonder whether I should wake him. I'm only going downstairs to grab a glass of water.

I leave his room, then pause at the top of the stairs and listen to the blend of soft music and quiet snoring from below. My eyes sweep across the room, landing on three people sprawled awkwardly on the pool table. I wince; that can't be comfortable. Empty beer bottles and cans litter the space. At the bar a few men sit hunched over their drinks. With a deep breath, I start my cautious descent, feeling the cool handrail under my fingertips. I just need to reach the kitchen, and then I can retreat back to Axle's room.

The men at the bar make my pulse accelerate. I try to creep by, but their gazes pierce me. One whistles, making me recoil. Perhaps I should have convinced Axle to come downstairs with me. I lower my head. Maybe if I ignore them, they'll get the hint.

I rush to the kitchen, where I search the cupboards for a glass that looks clean. I find a glass and fill it from the tap. I really don't want to walk by the men in the bar again. My hands shake as I grip the glass. I just need to get past them and get upstairs to Axle.

I exhale sharply and dash out of the kitchen and through the house while trying not to splash my water. I hear footsteps. My heart beats wildly. A large, intimidating man is blocking my way. I don't recognize him.

His eyes roam me with greedy delight. My stomach drops. "Can I please get past?" I murmur. I just need to get up the stairs.

"Come dance with me."

My grip around the glass tightens. I wait for him to move, but he doesn't, so I answer, "No," and try to sidestep him.

He leans down and grabs my hips.

"Let go," I say, my voice unsteady.

His hands tighten. "Just dance with me."

"Elena?" Axle is standing at the top of the stairs, his face set in stone.

The relief that washes over me eases the tightness in my chest. Axle's eyes are darting to me, the guy . . . His gaze turns deadly when he sees the guy's hands on my hips. The guy jerks his hands off me and takes a deliberate step away. I shuffle backward until my back is against the wall.

"Sorry, man," he blurts out, "I didn't know she was with you."

Axle races down the stairs with incredible speed. "I'm sorry, I'm sorry," the man pleads, but Axle doesn't hesitate. He tackles the man to the ground, the impact echoing on the wooden floor. With urgency, Axle straddles him, pulls back his arm, and delivers a punch that lands with a sickening crunch.

Startled by the sudden violence, I jump. My medication and the glass of water slip from my grasp. The glass shatters on the floor, breaking into tiny shards. The crash catches Axle's attention, and he stops and glances up at me. When he sees my concerned expression, he slowly rises. The guy underneath him rolls to his side, groaning and holding his nose.

Cash and Twitch rush in as Reaper storms down the stairs.

Axle takes cautious steps toward me. "Everything's

okay . . ." he says soothingly as the glass crunches under his boots.

"What happened?" Reaper booms.

The weight of the gaze of everyone in the room makes my skin prickle, but my throat tightens, leaving me unable to utter a single word.

"Piece of shit put his hands on Elena," Axle spits. He looks like he's holding himself back from going another round with the man on the floor.

Reaper's eyes cut to the man and his two friends, who have come over to help him up. "You three are never getting patched in . . . get out."

Axle wraps his arms around me. "I'm sorry," he says softly into my neck, his words muffled.

"Everyone out!" Reaper yells. Twitch and Cash start moving around the room, waking people up and telling those who are awake to leave.

Axle leans back and observes me. "Are you okay?"

My breathing is still heavy, but I nod. "I am . . . He just startled me." I couldn't decide what frightened me more: the man who believed it was acceptable to grab me like that or Axle's talent for rapidly switching from zero to death row.

"Can someone clean this mess up?" Axle yells.

"I'll do it," Mercedez says, then scurries away.

He looks down, bends over to pick up the pill bottle, and reads the label. He takes a step closer to me and gently asks, "Are these yours?"

"Yes."

He passes them to me. Mercedez gets to work with the broom, cleaning up the glass.

Axle frowns. "I'll pick you up so that you don't get cut by glass."

I nod, and he picks me up with ease. I wrap my legs around his waist.

"I've got you," he says as he walks through the mess to the kitchen. He sets my feet on the floor before he opens the fridge to pull out a bottle of water, which he passes to me. He peeks at the pill bottle in my hand, tilting his head. "What are they for?"

"It's my anxiety medication," I say before opening the lid and pulling out two tablets and taking them with a gulp of water.

Even though I'm wary of Axle, the deep frown on his face makes my heart contract. I go to him and touch his arm. "Please don't hurt someone like that again. It was a shock . . . to see you like that."

He blinks at me, then chuckles briefly. "You see my cut, yeah?" He points to the patch on his vest.

I bite my lip and nod.

"I won't let anyone touch you." He directs his attention to my bottle of tablets once more. "And now you're going to be scared to come back thanks to that trash."

Cash walks in and leans against the wall. "Are you okay?" he asks me.

"Yes, thanks." I'm not, but I appreciate his kindness in asking.

Reaper walks in. "No more parties for a while. I've had enough of randoms coming to our clubhouse." His eyes meet mine. "Did he hurt you?"

I shake my head.

Reaper turns to Axle, his eyes narrow. "I mean it. No more parties."

Axle is the one who organizes the parties . . . That doesn't sit well with me.

"Last night was all Viper, not me," Axle tells Reaper.

"I'll be sure to tell him that too, then."

"I'm going to go home," I say to Axle. I need some downtime. It's been chaotic.

Disappointment flashes in his eyes before he offers me a small smile. "Sure."

As we walk through the clubhouse, I bow my head. People are probably staring at me after what had happened earlier. When we get to Axle's bedroom, he leans against the doorway as I put my tablets away and hook my bag over my shoulder.

"You're not scared of me, are you?"

I pause, my eyes scanning his face. "I'm not scared of *you*. Just how you reacted."

He folds his arms across his chest. "He put his hands on you!" he says defensively. "I'm not one of the *boys* you would have hung around. I'm a man . . . a biker. I handle business, and I'm not letting a piece of shit hang-around make you feel unsafe in my own home."

I sigh. I was relieved he was there to protect me. He's right—he's not like anyone else I've met, and I should take that into account and accept that he won't react the same way either.

"Can I come back to your house with you?" he asks.

I smile at the knowledge that he still wants to spend time with me. "Yes, okay."

Once we reach the shed, I frown when I see my car's tight fit. "Can you reverse my car for me?"

"Pass me the keys," he says with a grin. "I'll move your car and ride behind you on my bike."

I move off to the side as he reverses my beat-up car. I still find his capability sexy. My car stands out among the lines of shiny motorcycles. The van is the only other thing that looks as crappy as my car.

I walk over to the driver's side as he's getting out. He stifles a laugh.

"What?"

"A good Christian girl like you listening to a woman rapping about pussy."

I cringe at the word, then glance at my car. "It doesn't sound as bad when she's rapping."

He steps aside, lets me get in, and then closes the door. "I'll see you at yours."

"Ride safely," I'm quick to reply. The motorcycle might be fun, but it's still dangerous.

He pauses and gives me a strange look and then a slight nod.

As I'm easing away, I hear the rumble of his bike. It isn't long until I pull up outside my house and he's parked behind me.

When I step out of the car, I notice that the driveway is full of cars. Everyone's home. I patiently wait for Axle to get off his bike before I say, "We can go somewhere else."

With a slight head shake, he asks, "I thought you wanted to come back to your house?" He looks confused.

I peer back at the driveway. "I think everyone's home, though."

He shrugs. "So?"

"I'm not sure how they are going to react, and if the guys are here, I don't want them annoying you."

His head inches back as his eyes grow cold. "You live with guys?"

I cringe. "Not technically."

"What do you mean, not technically?"

I'm not one to cause conflict, but I'm not going back to the negativity I had to deal with when I lived with my parents. "They stay here occasionally because *their* girlfriends live here with me."

"Like that matters," he says with attitude. "They're still staying the night here."

I put my hand up. "Stop." I straighten my back, standing

up taller. "I live with a group of friendly people and . . ." I pout. "At least I've never walked in on them having sex."

His lip twitches as if he's fighting a smile. "Okay, okay," he says, but I'm not entirely convinced. He puts his arm around my shoulders like he always does and pulls me into him while we head to the house. He allows me room to walk in first.

I hear voices coming from the living room. "Shh . . . Shh . . . they're coming inside."

I tilt my head toward my roommates. "I'll introduce you."

He grasps my hand and links our fingers together. I smile at him, but his body's still stiff.

When we walk into the living room, all my roommates and their boyfriends are sitting wide-eyed on the couch. "Hey . . . this is Axle," I say and look back at him.

Axle is no longer his playful self. He's drawn himself up to his full, intimidating height. He gives them a "hey" and a chin lift in greeting. I squeeze his hand.

I point to each roommate as I say their name. "That's Lucy, Jeremy, Lia, Jasmine, Cindy, and Justin."

"We've met," says Jasmine.

Axle tilts his head and looks at her. "Have we?"

The boys cackle. "Ouch!" one says. Jasmine throws a pillow at him.

I pull Axle toward the kitchen and let them talk among themselves. "Do you want a drink?"

"Nah . . ." he says. He stands by the kitchen counter. "I'll have food, though. What are you cooking for me, babe?"

I laugh.

He pulls a comical face. "It's a serious question," he deadpans. Him and his precious food.

"Sorry, I can't cook."

His face drops and he points to the front door. "Get out."

I break into a smile. "What . . .? Why?"

"You can't cook. I want a refund."

I lean over and playfully swat his arm. *Cheeky!* "How about some peanut butter on toast?" I suggest with a hopeful smile.

He lets out an exaggerated sigh. "Yeah, I suppose that'll do."

I know he's joking, and I chuckle. I pull out the bread and the peanut butter.

"Why do you take the tablets?" he asks, his voice laced with a hint of sadness.

I pause as I put the bread into the toaster. "It's complicated."

"Uncomplicate it for me. Help me understand."

"I've been taking them since high school. My parents had high expectations of me to excel at school—and I put a lot of pressure on myself too. I think by the end of it I just burned myself out, and if you haven't noticed . . ." I look down before making eye contact again. "I'm shy and super awkward. I struggle socially and with groups of people, but I'm trying."

He steps over to me, grips the back of my head, and gives me a chaste kiss on the lips. He peers over my shoulder. "I think my toast is burning."

It takes a moment to understand what he's saying. I whirl and press the button. The toast pops up. It's only slightly blackened—we saved it just in time.

I put our toast on plates, then spread the peanut butter. We eat in a comfortable silence, though as per usual he takes next to no time to eat. "How was it?" I say, trying not to laugh.

"Legendary," he says with a chef's kiss.

I laugh and playfully swat him again. "Liar."

My phone buzzes in my pocket. I pull it out to see Mom calling. "Hello, Mom?"

Axle leans in closer to me.

"I'm just calling to say I've booked a reservation for dinner for your birthday."

I frown, not sure whether I want to go back home, but I guess it's better than celebrating it by myself. "Okay, thanks."

"Henry will also be home to visit his parents, so I've invited their family to join us."

My eyes bulge. I take a few steps away from Axle.

"We're not together anymore," I say quietly. I get along with Henry and his family, but it's my birthday and I'd prefer them not to be there. It should be my choice, not hers.

"I can't comprehend why you ended it with him," she says in a clipped tone.

I groan, not wanting to have this discussion. "I'm busy . . . I'll talk to you another time."

"Too busy for your own mother," she pipes up.

Well, it's not like she's been checking up on me, but I bite my tongue. "Yes, Mom, I'm busy right now. Bye," I say before disconnecting the phone.

"What the fuck is up with your mom? She sounds like a bitch."

I flinch but don't disagree. "She's always been full-on and controlling like that. Just not as bad. It's only become a problem now because they don't agree with any of my life choices after school."

"You need to set her straight. Don't put up with her bullshit, with treating you like that . . . What are you doing for your birthday?"

I sigh. "Going out for dinner, I guess."

He snorts. "With your ex?"

I look down at the ground, then back to him. "I guess so."

His eyebrows are raised high. "Well . . . that ain't happening, and who cares what your parents want you to do? What do you want to do?"

I don't think anyone's asked me that before. I shrug. "I don't know. I haven't given it much thought."

"You tell me what you want to do, and I'll make it happen."

My heart flutters. Henry never offered that. In fact, no one ever has. I don't know Axle that well and he's offering. It's a big deal.

I glance down at my phone. "I've got to get ready for work." My buzz fades. I don't want to leave him.

"Then I might start heading out. I'll see you tonight."

My smile grows. "I'm seeing you tonight, am I?" I ask coyly.

He grabs my arms and swings me around until I'm in front of him. "Damn straight you are." He kisses me and smiles against my lips. "I better go, before I decide to keep you tied to me."

I laugh, though I don't know whether he's serious or not. I wouldn't put it past him. As I walk away, I feel a shooting slapping pain on my ass, making me gasp and jump. I turn to face him with narrowed eyes. My first thought is, *How dare he disrespect me.* My second thought is, *Oh, I actually didn't mind it.*

He groans. "Don't look at me like that." He shakes his head. "I'm out of here."

ELEVEN

PRETTY LITTLE LIE

Axle

I'M AN ASSHOLE . . . IF I WERE A BETTER PERSON, I'D QUIT THIS now, but I'm not a better person. I've gotten a taste of her, and now I'm hooked. She's addictive, and I feel high every second I'm with her. Every moment with her feels exhilarating, like an intoxicating rush I can't escape. I'm not giving that up. I'm going to hang on to her as long as I can.

I thought she'd be boring, make me go to church, get angry every time I cussed, but she's a cool chick. She's like a breath of fresh air. I don't kiss women, but my mouth waters thinking about the taste of her. Those seductive eyes when I smacked her ass . . . *oh shiiit*. I just wanted to drag her ass up to her room, but she's not that type of girl. The thought of getting between those creamy thighs, devouring her . . . giving her what she's never experienced . . . I'm hard. I groan . . . My dick and balls are going to be aching every time I see her.

I gently run the cloth over my bike. The front door creaks open, and Viper's voice cuts through the air. "Axle, church!"

After draping the cloth over the bucket, I walk inside. The door swings open to reveal Viper waiting for me.

"What happened this morning?" he asks.

I grind my teeth. "Some drunk put his hands on Elena. She looked terrified, and I lost it . . ." I shake my head, trying to get the frightened look on her face out of my mind. I feel an immediate impulse to hit that guy again.

"I gathered"—he smirks—"by the blood that was pouring out of the guy's nose that he had pissed you off."

"He's lucky that's all he got. I should see if Twitch knows where he lives."

Viper puts his hand on my shoulder. "Let it go. They aren't allowed back in the clubhouse. I haven't seen you like that since the early days . . . Are you all right, brother?"

As in when I was out of control . . .

We walk toward church. "She's a sweet girl. The thought of someone putting their hands on her or scaring her . . . . I wanted to rip the guy to shreds." The need to protect her has me clenching my fists.

"I get it. I've just never seen you act like that over a chick."

I've never felt the need to.

We put our phones in the bowl outside church before we walk inside and take our seats. Reaper sits at the head of the table.

Once the door is closed, Reaper, our president, begins. "Cash, how are our finances?"

"Fridges are stocked, bills paid. Everything's good on our end," Cash replies.

Reaper nods and looks around the table. "I want to make it clear, like I said this morning, no more parties." Reaper holds eye contact with me and Viper.

Viper frowns and turns to me. I shrug. I no longer give a shit. Not after this morning.

"One of our fighters approached me asking if he could be a prospect," Reaper declares.

"Who?" I ask.

"Theo," Reaper replies. "The young man they call Rage who's been winning all the fights."

"He's been killing it," says Viper.

"The kid looks young. How old is he?" asks Bomber. We won't take on anyone as a prospect under eighteen, but the guy is a ruthless fighter. I'll give him that.

"Nineteen," says Twitch.

I raise a brow at him. Of course he knows. He's the computer guy—he can find out anything. Thanks to him, I found Elena.

"Did you look into Rage?" Reaper asks.

Twitch nods. "Certainly did."

"Has anything turned up in his background?"

"No, he only recently got out of school. He was brought up by a single mom. He has a younger brother. No red flags."

"He's a fucking good fighter. He'll bring in some serious coin," says Viper.

"If you're in agreement with Rage being a prospect, raise your hand," says Reaper.

Everyone around the table does.

Reaper glances at Cash. "Can you organize a War Brothers MC cut with a prospect patch for him?"

Cash nods. "Will do, Pres."

Reaper looks at me. "We've got a run soon. Axle, can you organize the best route to get there?"

"Sure, I've already started." I need to ensure we can get the shipment of pot there in the quickest time while avoiding public attention and the police. That includes traveling at night and paying off police officers in some counties to ensure safe travels.

"Once we confirm a date and time, Bomber, can you please check with your uncle to ensure it won't pose any problems?"

Bomber nods, while I roll my eyes. Our town is pretty much owned by Bomber's uncle, who has a hand in everything. Bomber has to speak with him to move our shipment of pot through Crown Village and the surrounding towns. His uncle extorts us for a cut of our profits, as if he isn't rich enough. He owns a lot of businesses in town, and we must get the go-ahead so he can make sure the police won't give us any hassle.

It's not like we deal hard drugs to the people in town. We just grow pot and sell it to a couple of motorcycle clubs, and then they distribute it between their clubs. That and the illegal fights earn us money. We're tame compared to a lot of motorcycle clubs. Some of them do things that are a lot worse to earn money.

"Has anyone got anything else they want to bring to the table?" asks Reaper.

The room is quiet. Then Reaper slams down the gavel to show it's the end of church.

As I stand, I glance at Twitch. "I need you to do something for me."

"Axle," Reaper says, making me turn. "Can I talk to you?"

I smile. Judging by the intensity of his expression, I doubt it will be a good chat.

I turn back to Twitch. "I'll meet you at the computer room."

As I step over to Reaper, he asks, "What are you doing with that girl?"

I jerk my head back in surprise. "I don't know . . . I'm just getting to know her."

He raises a brow. "I heard about the bet between you and Viper. I'm telling you now, it will not end well for you or the girl."

Nothing I don't already know . . . but I'm not willing to give her up. "It's not just about the bet anymore." I like spending time with her.

He searches my eyes and gives me a slow nod. "A word of advice? Keep your emotions in check. She's attractive and is naturally going to draw attention. You can't lose control every time some man shows interest in her, and from what I saw, she wasn't just scared of the guy who touched her—she looked worried about how you reacted."

"Yeah, yeah, I will." *I'll try.* "But the man touched her."

"I know. The guy deserved it. I'm not saying not to protect her. Just keep yourself in check."

Reckless is my middle name. I give him a tight nod before I leave and go to the computer room to Twitch.

"Hey, man," I say.

Twitch spins around in his chair to turn his attention to me.

"Can you look into Elena's boss for me? Dig up some dirt. I don't like the guy, and I want to make sure it's safe for her to work there. There's something off about him . . . I just want to know what it is."

"Of course. Why, what are you thinking?"

Usually nothing bothers me, but I'm on edge after this morning. "Elena is too nice . . . too trusting. I don't want a repeat of this morning, so I want to check him out since he's working with her every day. I've just got a bad feeling about him."

I leave the room and start walking through the house. Perhaps I'm paranoid, but I've seen the way he gazes at her, and I know that look. He wants to bang her for sure. I growl in annoyance, then pause. *Why do I care so much?* I'm the one

Elena should run far away from, but I tell myself I'm just looking out for her. Elena's out of my league, but she doesn't think so or she wouldn't be hanging out with me.

Viper catches up with me. "Did Reaper give you a lecture about Elena?"

"Reaper just said I've got to keep my emotions in check." He has a point, but saying and doing are two completely different things. "As long as no one touches Elena"—or looks at her—"I'm sweet."

"I thought she was going to be a bit of fun for you. I honestly didn't think you'd last after the first date. I know you wanted to win the bet, but I thought you'd be bored out of your brain. That's why I took the bet. But after this morning, watching you lose it like that . . ." He shakes his head. "You two aren't good for each other. I can see it now. If anything happens to her, you're going to lose it."

I glare at him, my body tense. "Why does everyone suddenly have opinions about the girl I'm with? I'm not giving her up." Hell to the no.

"Because she's not like the other women you've been with. I don't see her being able to handle being in the clubhouse."

"She'll be fine, and it won't kill you to keep your dick in your pants when you're outside of your bedroom." And anyway, Elena's handled everything so far.

He sighs and looks past me. I turn to see Grace and Candy walking toward us. Now it's my turn to sigh. For fuck's sake . . . I wish everyone would just give me a break. Grace sways her hips as she walks to me with that same so-called seductive smile she always gives me.

"No!"

Both girls stop, their eyes wide.

"I'm not in the mood to deal with you right now." I look

directly at Grace. "Turn your ass around and go shake it at one of my brothers."

Grace gasps. "Why? The nun clearly isn't giving you any."

I turn to give Viper a pointed glare. He gave Elena the name that Grace is using now. He winces.

Grace pouts, crossing her arms over her chest. "Tell me I'm lying? She's never going to be enough for you . . . Uptight bitch."

My jaw clenches as I stride toward her. She swallows hard, taking a few steps back. "If I hear you"—I turn my deadly stare to Candy—"any of you disrespect Elena"—I look back at Grace—"I'll show you exactly what fucking rude *really* is." My voice is deep, the threat clear. "Then I'll ban you and you can go back to wherever the fuck you came from."

Grace mutters, "Asshole," as she turns and leaves, and it makes me smile. *Yes, yes, I am,* but I'm not putting up with her shit. She's a guest living in my home.

I take my phone out and check the time. I'm counting down the hours to see Elena. I'm strung out. I like pretending she's mine even though it's a pretty little lie.

"Axle."

I turn to Twitch.

"Come see what I found." The intensity in his eyes unsettles me. "It's not good man."

TWELVE
WHIPLASH

Elena

"WHAT'S UP WITH YOU TODAY?" MEL ASKS.

I peer up at her, then finish wiping the table before I speak. "I stayed the night at the clubhouse."

Her mouth falls open, and she just stares at me for a moment. "Really? How was it? You'll have to invite me next time!"

"It was eye-opening." To say the least.

She steps closer to me. "Why? What happened? What were all the men like?"

"They seemed normal at first. Men playing pool and a few people playing darts, but then I saw two people having sex out in the open on the couch." I wince at the flashback. "Then someone playing darts used a knife instead of a dart to win. It was crazy how good his accuracy was . . . kind of scary."

She lets out a deep sigh. "You're so lucky . . . I want to go so bad."

There's such yearning in her voice that I cock my head. "Then why don't you?"

"I've never been, and I'm not willing to take the risk of being kicked out. That's why I created your profile. Axle didn't accept my request on the dating app, so I hoped he would accept you and you'd be my in. Did you talk to any of the other bikers or . . .?"

So, she used me. "I met most of them. The MC men look intimidating but seem surprisingly nice and down-to-earth." Well . . . most of them.

I step over to the closest table and start wiping it down, then flinch when I remember what happened in the morning.

"What's wrong?" she asks, her curiosity obvious.

I blow out a long, drawn-out breath through my mouth. "In the morning after I woke up, I went to get some water—"

With wide eyes she cuts me off. "Did you have sex with him?"

"No," I clip out.

I open my mouth to speak, but she's not finished. "Why not? You're not going to keep him around by teasing him. He'll get sick of that in no time."

Frustration claws at me. "I told him I'm not going to have sex with him. He already knows how I feel about it." I know he's a biker, but not everything's about sex . . . *or is it?* I shake my head, dismissing the thought.

"As I was saying, when I woke up, I went downstairs to get some water. They must have had a party after we went to bed. Some people were still awake, though none of them had the War Brothers MC vests on. One guy grabbed me, trying to get me to dance, but when I said no, he wouldn't listen. Axle saw it, ran down the stairs, tackled the guy, and started punching him." Thinking back to the blood splattering makes me flinch.

"Oh wow. I wish a guy came to my defense like that."

"Axle was hurting the guy . . . because he touched me." A sliver of guilt pierces me.

She subtly rolls her eyes. "You were staying at a clubhouse full of bikers and people that like to party . . . What did you expect to happen if Axle saw you were getting hit on or hurt by a stranger? I think it's hot he came to defend you."

"I guess." He's a biker. He won't act like the people I'm used to being with, and I know that if I'm going to spend time with him, I need to make peace with that.

After I finish cleaning, I get ready to leave. "Elena." Cameron is waving me over from a hallway at the rear of the kitchen.

I walk in his direction. I've never been in this part of the restaurant. I see a room off the hallway to the right. An unsettling sensation begins to grow in my stomach. I pause at the door and look around the office.

Cameron is sitting behind his desk. He gestures at the chair opposite him, so I take a seat.

"How are you doing? Are you enjoying working here?"

I smile. "Yes, I'm learning new things on every shift." I'm proud that I haven't dropped any more trays of food and drink. It must be a new record for me. "The tips are great." So much better than my last job. "While we're here . . . would it be possible to take tonight off?" I need a break, and it would be great to relax and not have to worry about work.

He gives me a leisurely nod. "I can't see why not. Why don't you have tomorrow off too, since you've been working hard?"

Staying in pajamas all day to relax or exploring the town both sound great. "Thank you," I reply happily.

"Why don't you come out with me, Lucy, and our group of friends instead? You'll enjoy yourself."

And there it is . . .

"We're always at the beach, hanging out, going to parties. Before you say anything—it's just people our age hanging out, listening to music, and having a few drinks. You'll like it."

This time I force a smile. I'm sure he's just trying to be nice, but he keeps asking me, and it's starting to feel a little pushy. My smile might mask the slight discomfort I'm feeling, but it doesn't change the fact that his persistence is starting to wear on me.

"Just have a think about it."

"I will," I say and stand, striding to the door and into the hallway.

"Elena," Cameron calls out.

I turn and he moves toward me. I back away because he's too close and in my personal space.

"Why are you so hesitant about hanging out with us, but you'll hang out with a biker?"

The malice in his tone as he emphasizes the word *biker* makes me take another step back.

"Where is she?" a loud male voice booms.

I startle . . . Is that . . .? My boss gasps and darts into his office, closing the door. I suck in a breath and hurry out into the kitchen.

When Axle's eyes land on me, his shoulders fall. He strides to me, his face set and his jaw ticking. I rack my brain as I try to work out what's wrong with him, but nothing comes to mind.

"Where's your boss?" he asks, his wild eyes searching the kitchen. All the chefs have stopped cooking and are standing still, watching us wide-eyed.

"Let's talk outside," I say soothingly, hoping I can calm him down out there, though inside I'm raging. I want to know what has him so upset at my boss, but another part of me wants to yell at him for disrespecting me at work.

"You're quitting," he demands as we walk, further intensifying the searing burn of anger.

We stride out of the building, Axle ushering me out with a hand pressed against my lower back. I keep walking until we're beside my car. For someone so easygoing, he surely gets angry . . . or is it jealousy?

I whip around to face him. "What was that about?" I hiss.

He growls. "I knew your boss was shady." He looks at the restaurant, his top lip curling up. His eyes flick back to me. "Has he touched you?"

I freeze and stare at him mutely.

He turns and starts marching back to the restaurant, so I dash to him and grab his hand with both of mine, pulling him close to me. "No, he hasn't." He has touched me lightly, but he hasn't touched my bum or anything, which I think is what Axle is talking about.

He's clenching his other hand. "What's wrong?" I ask.

"He was accused of sexual assault but paid the girl off. You're no longer working here."

My stomach drops. I gulp. It makes sense now why I was uncomfortable. "Cameron hasn't done anything. I promise. I'm at work surrounded by other people." My eyes soften. "I need this job."

"No fucking way!" he says with a savage bite.

I nibble on my lip. "I hate that it happened to another woman, and it's wrong on so many levels, but I need this job," I whisper. "Independence is important to me. I need to have it. I'll start searching for other jobs in town, but I can't just leave this one. I need the money, and I've only just started. I don't know whether anyone would hire someone who just left their job when they haven't even been there for long."

He shrugs. "People quit all the time, and I've got money."

"First, I don't want your money. I want my own. Second, I moved here because I wanted to be independent. I know you're worried, but I can't leave . . . not yet, not until I have another job. And third, we're not together."

Axle stands tall. His face is still stern. He's not budging.

"I can't have someone trying to rule my life again . . . It's a deal-breaker for me."

With a brief shake of his head, he crosses his arms, making his biceps bulge. "First," he says, copying my tone but injecting more attitude, "you *are* my woman."

I can't stop my lips from curving into a slow smile. "Am I?" In the back of my mind, I know I should be alarmed, but I really like him, and that overrides any doubts.

He nods his head sharply. "Yeah, you are." He steps toward me and pulls me to his chest. I put my arms around his waist, but he's still rigid. He leans back, cups my face, and lifts my head. "With you going to work, I don't fucking like it. Your safety and my sanity are more important than a job."

I stand on my toes and wrap my arms around his shoulders. "I promise I'll keep looking for jobs," I say before my lips touch his in a tender kiss.

"As long as I pick you up and drop you off at work. And you can't be alone with him ever . . . or go to work when it's just you two."

"Bossy!"

He nods. "Sure am."

"I'm capable of driving myself, but yes, I promise I won't be alone with him."

The side of his lip twitches. "Are you staying over at mine tonight?"

"Uh . . ."

"There won't be any more strangers at the clubhouse," he's quick to respond.

A little relief filters through. I'd rather not be home, where my boss can show up unexpectedly. It makes me question how my roommates are friends with someone like that. "Okay, I'll get my things." I lean up on my toes. His eyes slightly soften, but there's still an edge to him.

I get in my car and glance at him, but he stands off to the side, waiting for me to drive off. I put my key in the ignition, but nothing happens. I take the key out and try again. It doesn't start. "Great . . ." I mutter, then open the car door. "My car just died. Can you check it out for me?"

He smirks, appearing thoroughly amused with himself. "It's so old. The parts will cost a fortune, and you'll probably just have to buy another car."

My stomach drops. I can't afford that. He opens the hood and looks at the engine. My head falls back against the head-rest. How will I manage to travel to work now? I refuse to move back home with my parents . . . I just can't.

When I hear the hood shut, I look up at Axle optimistically, but the shake of his head all but crushes my hope. "There's probably something wrong with your fuel pump. It seems I'm taking you to work every day now," he says proudly.

I stand, shut the car door, and lock it. "You must be happy that you're getting your own way."

"You bet I am," he replies with complete and utter smugness, but his cheeriness doesn't reach his eyes. He puts his arm around my waist and draws me closer, and exhales deeply. "We'll go to yours and pick up your clothes. You should bring a big bag. I don't know how long the part and fixing the car will take."

"Okay, but I have to make it to every shift on time."

"I can do that."

I peer around. "Where's your bike?"

He points to the van a few parking spaces away. I'm grateful. That means I don't have to carry my bag on my back.

"We'll grab some dinner on the way," he suggests.

After we arrive at the clubhouse, he parks the van in the shed. I thought he'd be happy I'm staying with him, but he still seems distant. He was quiet on the way over. He takes my bag from the back seat and takes my hand.

Carrying our takeout in my other hand, I walk toward the house. I listen for loud music or any signs of a party, but there are none. My body becomes rigid and I cower as we walk inside, but when I steal a glance at the living room, I don't see anyone having sex. I exhale gratefully.

"Disappointed, are you?" Viper is at the bar, smiling widely, a beer in his hand.

"I'd say I'm relieved," I reply, making him chuckle.

"The fights are on tonight. All of them will be out," says Axle. He tugs on my hand, so I follow him up the stairs.

When we walk into his room, he sets down my bag by his wardrobe. I frown. "What's wrong?"

"Nothing," he says, but his voice is emotionless and he's not making eye contact.

I know something is wrong. I'm getting whiplash from his mood changes today.

"You want to go and grab a drink with dinner?" he asks, tilting his head toward the door.

I release a ragged breath and follow him out, down the stairs.

"Go take a seat in the living room, and I'll get us some drinks. What do you want?"

I want him to be happy. "Just water, thanks."

He walks toward the kitchen while I walk into the living room, where all four sweet butts are seated with Twitch. All of them focus their attention on me. Grace huffs, then rolls her eyes. She peers around me—I assume she's looking for Axle

—and then stands and gestures toward the couch. "Here you go, your highness."

Heaviness cloaks me. I hate conflict.

She storms away. "Grace," Vera calls out and then runs after her. Mercedez sighs, while Candy smiles up at me.

"Take a seat," Twitch says, gesturing to the seats the girls just vacated.

Axle comes up behind me and sits down, so I cautiously take a seat next to him. He puts a bottle of water next to me and I pass him his burger and fries.

"Are you going to the fight tonight?" Twitch asks, looking from me to Axle.

Axle takes a big bite of his burger and shakes his head.

"Are you going?" Mercedez asks Twitch. She's lying next to him, rubbing his leg.

"If they want me to, I will, but I'd rather stay here."

Mercedez smiles up at him.

I wonder if Twitch and Mercedez are a couple. They act like they are. It makes me wonder about me and Axle. Are all bikers who are in relationships with women doing what they want—having their cake and eating it too? I hope not.

"What are the fights?" I ask.

All eyes go to Axle, like they're waiting for him to answer.

"The MC runs illegal fights."

My shoulders tense at the word *illegal*. "Why?"

"It earns us money," Axle answers bluntly.

I eat a few chips while I think about that. "Do *you* fight?"

"None of us do."

I'm left wondering whether I've said something wrong. I relax on the couch, happy to know it's not Axle fighting. I briefly wonder about the MC's additional earnings, but I push the thought aside. I don't think I want to know.

"Well, the prospect will be," Twitch says.

"He isn't wearing our patch yet," Axle replies.

"What's a prospect?" I ask.

"A guy who wants to be a full patched member of the club but he has to prove himself first. Later on, we vote on if we want to patch him in," Axle answers.

"I've heard he's handsome," Candy says.

"Ooh . . . I can't wait to meet him," says Mercedez excitedly.

Twitch doesn't bat an eye at Mercedez's interest. I can't grasp how they can do that. They really must be with whoever they want at any time. I don't know how they don't get jealous . . . but then I think back to Grace. That could be why she's so upset with me. She was with Axle and envies me spending time with him. It all makes sense.

I watch a movie with them about a huge killer shark and a male hero that saves the day. After the credits roll, I hear the deep voices of the MC men. They're all heading for the front door. "Are they going to the fights now?" I ask.

"Yeah," Axle replies.

"I need to go to the bathroom. Can you point me in the right direction?" I ask him. I don't really need to go—I just need some space. Tension's rolling off Axle in waves.

"Mercedez, can you show Elena where the downstairs bathrooms are?"

Mercedez pouts and reluctantly gets up.

Oh crap! "It's okay, just tell me where it is."

Mercedez ignores me, so I follow her down the hallway. She points in the direction of the bathroom. I pause outside the door when I hear Grace's and Vera's voices inside.

"No more parties because of her. Who does she think she is? Axle was taken from me, now other men aren't allowed here anymore. For what . . . a guy touched her, who cares. She's not an ol' lady. The nun should go back to wherever she came from. She doesn't belong here." I can tell by the voice it's Grace speaking.

I flinch. That proves my theory. Nun? *Ouch!*

"I agree," says Vera. "But I think Reaper and a few of the men don't like the parties, bringing people they don't know into the clubhouse. I think it was a long time coming, but don't worry. Elena's not going to be here long. As soon as Axle's done with her, he'll be yours again."

I backpedal, regretting my decision to leave Axle. My chest aches. Grace sounds hurt and angry.

"I just don't get what the big deal is about her," Grace says. "She's got small tits. She's practically a virgin saint. He liked it when we fucked, and he fucked me hard. There's no way she's allowing him to do that to her."

Another blow to my chest, but this one hurts more.

Mercedez walks into the bathroom and clears her throat. I hear the soft hum of voices but can't make out what they are saying. Grace and Vera walk out, glaring at me as they pass by. Mercedez is walking out as I'm about to walk in. "What do you think about me and Axle?" I ask her.

She gazes at me with sympathy. "You sound like a nice girl, but . . . they have a point. You don't fit in here, and Axle is Axle."

My heart sinks.

"For your own self-preservation, I'd consider seeing someone outside of the MC. Grace really likes him, and I can't see her letting him go easily."

My shoulders fall. "Thanks for your honesty."

After I take a moment, I walk back to the living room, though I'm dragging my feet, feeling deflated by what the women said. I try my best to shake it off. When I meet Axle's gaze, I say, "I might go rest for a while."

"Are you alright?" asks Axle, frowning.

I glance at Mercedez, but quickly divert my gaze back to Axle, giving him a tight smile. "I'm fine."

Mercedez stands and grabs Twitch's hands in hers, pulling

him up. "Let's go lay down too," she says, her tone rich with innuendo.

We follow them out of the living room, but once we get to the far side of the room, Mercedez pushes Twitch against the wall and kisses him. In slow motion they swivel around, and Mercedez's arm falls back. She hits the motorcycle that's on the podium in the wall.

As it falls, I launch myself and catch it against my shoulder so that it doesn't crash to the ground. It's heavy, and pain radiates from the point of impact. A few seconds later Axle is pushing the bike upright. He carefully checks the bike for damage.

"Oh shit, we're sorry," Twitch blurts. Wariness is etched on his face, and he and Mercedez take a step back.

"Watch what you're fucking doing!" Axle lashes out, but the fear in his eyes is unmistakable. His heavy breaths pain me, so I gently grab his hand in mine and pull him away from them, through the house and into his bedroom.

Axle sits down on the bed and puts his head in his hands. We're silent as I kneel in front of him and undo his laces. His eyes are soft. He lifts first one leg and then the other so that I can tug his boots off.

His hands fall from his face as I stand up. He encircles me with his arms and pulls me between his legs. "It means a lot; you saved my bike tonight."

The vulnerability in his voice and his adoring gaze makes my eyes glassy. Clearing my throat, I run my fingers through his thick hair. "I know how much it means to you." I appreciate being privy to his past.

"I've been a cranky dick." His brows knit together. "Sorry, my head's not in a good place."

"Do you want to talk about it?"

"The thought of you going to work . . ." He shakes his head. "The more I think about it the angrier I get."

Remorse weighs heavily on my chest, so I lean down and give him a gentle kiss on the lips. "It won't be for long." It seems as though everything is against us and we are in constant battle with the rest of the world.

I step away from him and pull my pajamas out of my bag. I'm not sleeping in my clothes again. I clear my throat and give him a pointed look. The side of his lip lifts in a smirk, making me feel lighter. His smile is contagious. He slowly covers his eyes with his hands to give me some privacy.

I change into my pink satin pajama set. As I'm doing up the buttons on the pajama top, I glance at Axle. His dark hazel eyes are filled with lust and hold me captive as they travel slowly from my head to my toes, like he's committing what he's seeing to memory. When his eyes meet mine, they hold a promise of passion, which makes my heart hammer. I avert my gaze and busy myself with folding and repacking my clothes. I sense his eyes stalking me as I make my slow journey into the bed beside him, feeling a mix of butterflies and giddiness from the way he looks at me.

Axle slides his arms out of his vest, kicks off his jeans, and pulls his shirt over his head, revealing his tanned and taut skin, which is stretched over muscle. My eyes greedily study his body. My hands twitch—I crave to touch him—before my eyes land on his face, where I see a knowing grin. He knows I'm checking him out.

Axle's a storm of charisma and chaos, but I can't fight the feelings I have for him. He hides behind jokes and laughter, but behind his tough exterior, he bleeds like the rest of us.

He shuffles into bed next to me. My skin breaks out in goosebumps from the way his warm skin touches mine. I'm lying on my back, while he lies on his side, facing me.

"Why do you kiss me if you said that you don't kiss women?"

He smirks. "I seem to break all my rules with you."

I chew my lip, half smiling at his declaration.

He pulls the blanket down and runs his fingertips over my stomach, on top of my pajamas. My eyes close.

"Where did the motorcycle hurt you?" he asks softly.

My eyes connect with his adoring ones. I lift my hand to my shoulder.

With infinite gentleness, he places open-mouth kisses down my neck, eliciting a moan from me. His lips travel across my collarbone in deliberate, soft movements. He pulls at the neck of my pajamas, revealing my shoulder, where he presses a soft lingering kiss on the tender spot where the bike landed on me. My heart races wildly at his tenderness and at how he treasures my body.

"Were you hurt anywhere else?" he asks in a low, husky voice.

My breathing is heavy. It was mostly my shoulder, but I want him to go further, so I point to my lower stomach. His hands brush against my top and his eyes fixate on mine. He slides his hand beneath the bottom of my top and gradually lifts it higher. He watches me intensely, as if giving me a chance to say no, but I give him a brief nod because I desperately need his touch.

As his hand touches my breast, my thighs clench together. He massages one with his large, warm hand. Desire shoots through me. He pushes up my top and leans over, feasting on me. Sucking, pinching, teasing my nipple until my head falls back in pleasure. He plants open-mouth kisses down my stomach, making me shiver. He presses another lingering kiss to my lower stomach, where I said the bike caught me.

He props himself up on an elbow and lifts his head, his eyes surveying mine as his fingers delicately dance back and forth across my skin at the top of my shorts. His eyes search mine, and I brazenly spread my legs. My eyes are begging. I want more. Then his fingers made their way over my shorts.

"Are you a virgin?" he asks in a gravelly voice.

I can't speak, so I shake my head.

He growls. "I hate that some's had you before I have." His possessiveness edges on my raw ache. His hand slides under my shorts. I gasp, heart thumping. His hands go to my core and his finger teases my opening. I tense as his finger enters me, but as his lips meet mine, I relax. I trust him.

He slips in another thick finger, filling me, stretching me, and drags them slowly in and out. Pleasure courses through me. His tongue becomes more frenzied as his fingers thrust in and out, picking up speed. My back arches off the bed as I silently beg Axle to push me over the edge.

I've brought myself to orgasm before. Three-pump Henry never did it for me. When Axle's thumb meets my clit, I buck as it swirls in slow circles. My breaths come short and quick. Throwing my head back, I clutch the bed sheets. Pulling back, he watches me as I writhe under his touch.

"Come on my fingers," he demands as he increases the pressure on my clit. My ears are ringing. I struggle to draw in air.

"Let go and come for me, baby." The deep rumble of his voice and the added pressure of his thumb splinter my last shred of restraint. My muscles contract and release as spasms throw me into bliss. Lights dance behind my eyelids as I ride the waves of ecstasy, one after another, until I lie limp.

My eyes flutter open. His pupils are so dilated that his eyes are almost black, but there's a hint of a smile on his lips. "You're gorgeous when you come."

I glance down at his throbbing erection, my hand instinctively moving toward it. He tightly grasps my wrist. "Tonight is about you."

A new ache starts. I want him inside me. He lifts the fingers that were inside me and puts them to my lips, so I open, and he slides them into my mouth. Without hesitation I suck on his fingers, tasting myself, not caring.

He kisses me once more, this time slow and deliberate, each movement tender and full of warmth. With the gentle pressure of his lips, the slight tilt of his head, and the way his eyes soften when he looks at me, I know nothing could ever compare to the way he makes me feel.

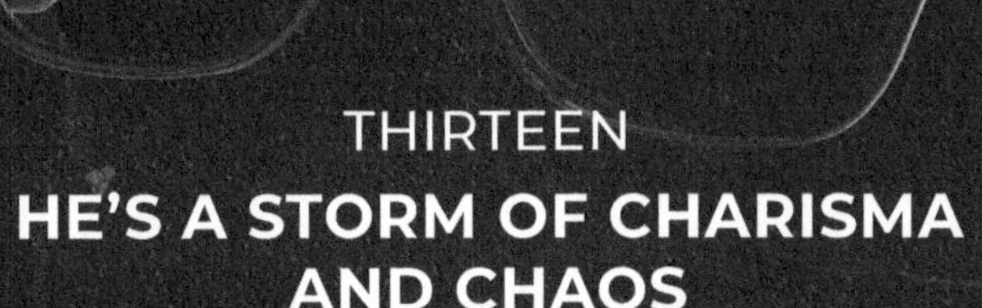

THIRTEEN

HE'S A STORM OF CHARISMA AND CHAOS

Elena

LAST NIGHT I LAY AWAKE LONG AFTER AXLE'S BREATHING LEVEL out. I think I've only had a few hours' sleep. His arms are still as tightly around me as they were when he fell asleep. His vulnerability bled through when Victor's bike fell, and seeing him tormented because I'm working at a place he doesn't perceive as safe stirs up inner turmoil.

I told him I wouldn't have sex with him, but I think I was trying to convince myself of that. There's been no pressure from him, and he seems happy to just spend time with me. That only makes me want him more. I can't help but compare him to my ex. Henry was a three-pump kind of guy, and I'm convinced that Axle isn't like that. The thought shoots straight to the juncture between my thighs, making me wiggle my butt.

"I wouldn't be doing that if I were you," a deep, sleepy voice murmurs behind me, making me smile.

"And if I do?" I tease. My mouth slams shut. *Who am I?*

His arms tighten around me. "If you want something, babe . . ."—his husky voice drifts off for a moment—"all you've got to do is tell me."

"I'll keep that in mind."

When he rubs himself against me, his hard thickness presses into my behind. My breathing deepens and I shiver with lust. I'm desperate to have sex with him, but the warnings I've gotten from everyone give me pause. I shuffle over to get out of bed, until big arms lunge and swoop around me, pulling me back into his chest, making me laugh.

"Nah, you're staying here with me, baby girl," he says seductively. His voice is tinged with playfulness.

My phone rings, so I jokingly smack his arm. "I've got to get my phone."

His arms tighten. "No, you don't."

"Please, Axle," I say, trying to keep the amusement out of my voice.

"Beg again for me," he purrs.

"Axle!" I warn, then he chuckles and lets go. I reach over quickly and grab my phone. It's Mel calling.

"Hello," I answer.

"Oh, hey," she says. "Someone mentioned you have today off."

"Yes," I reply slowly as Axle shuffles closer to me. "I do."

"Any chance we can swap shifts?"

I let out a sigh. I really wanted the day off.

Axle snatches my phone from my hand. As I'm about to object, he says into the phone, "No, she's not changing shifts."

He pauses while staring at me, then disconnects the call and passes me my phone.

I drill my displeased eyes into him. "You shouldn't have said that."

He gazes at me with one brow raised. "You let people treat

you like shit. If you're not willing to stand up for yourself, I will."

My heart seizes, and I smile at him. He's right. I probably would have given in and said yes to swapping shifts. It's nice to know someone's looking out for me.

The aroma of bacon wafts through the room, making Axle sit up straight. With a long moan, he rubs his hands together. "Are you ready for breakfast?" he asks.

I smile at his eagerness for food. "Certainly."

We both get out of bed, and as I walk to the door, he strides forward and stands directly facing me, blocking the door. He directs a sharp glance at me.

"What's wrong?" I ask.

He tuts. "Hell no. You're not leaving this room until you're wearing something . . ."—he gives my shorts a long stare—"something that covers more of this up." He squeezes my thighs.

I try to hide a smile at his overprotectiveness. I take one step to the side of him, making out like I'm trying to get past him and to the door. With one quick movement, he picks me up, steps over to the bed, and throws me down. I bounce as I land on the mattress and squeal with laughter.

"Don't test me, baby girl," he warns, then picks up his shirt from last night and throws it at me.

"There . . . wear that. It should cover more of your skin."

I get off the bed, stand, and pull his shirt over my head. It smells so damn good. The hem of the shirt falls below my knees. It covers more skin, but I look like a mess in it.

He steps toward me, grabs a fistful of his shirt, and abruptly yanks me to him until I'm glancing up into intense stormy eyes. "You look so fucking sexy in my shirt," he says before briefly crashing his lips to mine. I love how he takes control. His lips curve into a smile against mine. "Let's get some food. I'm starving to death."

I chuckle as he takes my hand. It's quiet when we descend the stairs, but while we navigate through the house and toward the kitchen, I hear voices outside. Axle leads me out the back door. Everyone is sitting at a long wooden table in the back yard. Platters of food have been set out along the center of the table. I recoil—everyone is staring at us. I give them a tight smile as a blush creeps up my face.

Grace and Vera are sitting together between Reaper and Candy. Grace says something to Vera and they both stand, their chairs scraping back. With heads held high, they grab their plates and walk past us. I haven't been disrespectful or suggested they can't be near Axle and me. They've made it clear they don't want to be around me.

Axle tugs on my hand, and we sit in the chairs Grace and Vera vacated. With Axle now seated next to Reaper, I sit next to Candy, who gives me a small smile. Axle loads his plate with bacon and eggs, toast, and hash browns. I follow his lead but dish up only one-third of his plate of food.

"What?" he asks me.

My eyes flick from his plate to his face. "Nothing," I murmur. I smile, wondering where all the food goes, because he's fit.

There's chatter around the table.

"Nice shirt," Viper muses.

I peer down at the black War Brothers MC T-shirt that's hanging off me.

"Yes," Axle answers for me. "She looks hot in it." Then his eyes narrow. "You take your flirty eyes off her."

Viper chuckles. "I haven't seen this overprotective boyfriend side of you." He raises his brow. "I must say, it's highly amusing."

The chatter around the table changes to a lingering silence. I sense everyone's eyes on me, but I calmly savor my meal and focus on my plate. I look up just in time to see a slice of toast, tossed by Axle, hit Viper in the head, which makes Viper laugh even harder.

Candy inches close to me. "Are you two in a relationship?" she asks quietly.

I slowly nod at her.

She cringes before she smiles. "Congratulations."

"What's wrong?" I ask warily.

"Oh . . . ah . . ." She lowers her voice to a whisper. "I guess I'm just shocked that out of all the MC members, it's Axle that's in a relationship. Like him . . . of all people."

"Aren't you with Viper?" I ask.

She frowns. "I wish . . . well, not yet anyway."

I chew my toast, my mind drifting off, wondering why everyone is so surprised by the way Axle acts around me. Is it because he likes me more than others . . . or is there something else I'm missing? And why has no other biker got a partner? It strikes me as odd.

"When are you checking the bikes?" Reaper asks Axle.

"Today," Axle replies.

Reaper nods. Even sitting down, he's an imposing man. He has broad shoulders and carries himself with authority.

My eyes wander over the table to Bomber. He has black hair and a thick beard. Every time I've seen him, he's always seemed crabby and in his own world.

Cash is next, and there's a noticeable ease in his demeanor compared to the others. He offers a genuine smile, his eyes crinkling warmly, and I find myself mirroring his expression. His calm presence makes me feel more comfortable and at ease.

Twitch sits next to him, with Mercedez on his other side. She seems to be by his side all the time.

Demon is last. His skin is covered in tattoos that extend all the way to his neck. He sits back casually in his chair, observing. He rarely speaks, but there's something not right about him. I watch him flick open a switchblade and then press the lock on the bolster before snapping the blade back into the frame. I shiver and shuffle closer to Axle.

After breakfast, as we're leaving the table, Axle asks, "Mind if I take a couple of hours to inspect the motorcycles? I want to make sure they're running smoothly for our ride."

I smile. "Yes, okay."

He grabs my hand and pulls me through the house, outside, and to the shed. He walks toward the back, where there's a workbench with tools set out and a stack of tires next to it. The space in front of the workbench is stained with oil. I lean on a table while he goes out the back and wheels one of the large black motorcycles into the space.

"When will you start working on my car?"

"I've been too busy." He grins.

I scoff. "You haven't been too busy while I've been here."

"Some pretty little lady's been taking up all my time."

I chuckle. "Can I ask you something?" I have a lot more questions than one.

He pauses, looks up at me, and then shrugs. "Go for it."

"Why aren't the other MC members married or in relationships?"

His head falls back as he cackles loudly. His laughter echoes through the shed. I stare at him, waiting for a response, but he carries on laughing. The MC men are a bunch of good-looking guys, and from what I've seen, the women go crazy over them.

He sighs, smiling. "Oh, you're serious? Okay, so let me give you the rundown. Viper's pretty and he knows it. Scores heaps of chicks but has Candy on the side. She'll hover over him and take whatever he has to give her."

I frown at Candy being Viper's last choice. It's sad.

"Reaper, our president, has sex with Vera and is pretty picky with women. He's too busy focusing on leading our club." Axle chuckles to himself. "He won't let any woman stay the night in his bed, which I find damn funny. So every night they have sex, Vera must leave afterward. You should see the sour look on her face, but Reaper has rules."

Axle takes a breath. "Cash . . . he has sex to pass the time. I've never seen him interested in anyone. He won't admit it, but he's clearly not over his ex. She must have done something terrible. He's usually such a chill guy, but whenever she's mentioned in conversation, he goes cold as ice.

"Bomber, the angry-looking man," he says mockingly, "with the I'm-so-serious-every-second-of-every-day vibe has ex-girlfriend drama too. Bomber won't have sexy time with anyone but escorts because he's that devoted to her. Pretty lame . . ."

I think Bomber is sweet in that way.

"Twitch is having a fling with Mercedez, but we think he has a hard-on for Reaper's sister Milly, which is funny because it will never ever happen."

"Why not?" I ask curiously.

"Because she's *Reaper's* sister, the one he's protected and supported since they were young. And Milly's shown no interest in anyone at the clubhouse. Twitch needs to get that out of his mind."

I bop my head in understanding.

"Then we have Demon. The rumor is he goes to the city for sex. I'm not sure what he gets there that he can't get here. Probably some kinky shit. He's a pretty closed-off guy. I think only Reaper knows his story. I don't know what woman would go for a sociopath anyway."

"Do you think something bad happened to him and that's why Demon is the way he is?" Scary as hell.

Axle's smile fades. "We've all had bad things happen to us, but sometimes it's like there's nothing behind Demon's eyes. He's always been loyal to the club and has done whatever has been asked of him. I know without a doubt that if I need him, he'll be by my side, no questions asked."

They might be bikers, but I find myself fascinated by their morals and ethics. If anything, I've learned that the MC is about loyalty, friendship, and sacrifice. I decide to lighten the mood, so I tease, "You know a lot about your friends' love lives. You're a gossip."

His grin spreads wide. "Oh yeah, baby," he says as he steps back over to the bike with a tool in his hand.

I remain quiet as I watch him. I have no idea what he's doing, though he appears confident.

"Can you go over to the corner of the table? There's a dusty black stereo. Can you turn it on? That should turn on the radio."

After I turn it on for him, I say, "I have another question." I try to keep the anxiety out of my voice.

I obviously fail, because he says, "This isn't going to be a good question, is it?"

I puff out a breath of air. "Did you have anything going on with Grace?"

He laughs. "We used to have sex . . . nothing else."

Unease cloaks me. He just used her . . .

"Don't give me those judgy eyes," he says with attitude, and when I look at him, his brow is raised. "She knew the deal. I ended the casual sex, and she's pissed."

"Angry at me, you mean . . ."

His face turns stern. "Has she said anything to you?"

"No." Just passive-aggressiveness every time we cross paths. I'm just going to be the bigger person. "So that's it between you and her?"

"Yes, I'd rather shut my dick in a car door than go back to that."

My hands fly to my mouth as I try not to laugh at his rude comment.

"This song is a fuckin banger," Axle says happily while he works on the bike.

"I'm Sexy and I Know It" by LMFAO plays in the background. He dances from side to side, swinging his hips, making me laugh. It's somehow sexy and goofy at the same time.

He lifts his shirt over his head, and my eyes bug out of my head. I can't get over his muscle definition. His jeans hang dangerously low on his hips, and I'm pretty sure he's not wearing anything underneath them. He has the body of a god, and I crave him. "I just want to . . ."

He freezes. When my eyes meet his, he prowls toward me and picks me up, his hands under my ass. I wrap my legs around his hips and our bodies press together. His eyes search mine. "What do you want?" he asks in an urgent, deep voice.

I'm tongue-tied and suffocating from his closeness, but I snake my arms over his shoulders. His mouth hovers over mine, his warm breath caresses my skin, but he doesn't move. I'm burning up without his lips on mine. My eyes flick to his lips and back to his eyes.

"I'll ask again, babe . . . What do you want?"

I want him with a desperation I've never felt before, but the words don't find their way out of my mouth. Instead, my body aches as he slowly lets me down onto my feet. Disappointment slices me. He cups my face in his hands, crushing his lips to mine. I thread my fingers through his thick hair while I demand entrance into his mouth, granting me a low rumble from his chest.

Our tongues spar. Every nerve ending lights up. As I pull his head down harder, he inches back, nipping at my lip, sending a bolt of pleasure down lower. Then he's smiling against my lips. As he pulls away, he runs his hands slowly down my cheeks. I squint at him while his eyes dance with mischief. I step back. Something seems suspicious. "What did you do?"

He cackles to himself. He grabs my chin, gives me a hard peck on the lips, looks me dead in the eye, and says, "You look sexy with grease on your face, babe."

"You didn't," I say, but the smugness all over his face already answers his question for me. I step over to him and whack him. "This better come off!"

He shrugs. "Maybe . . . maybe not."

I look down at my jeans, then try to turn around to see if there's grease on my ass from him holding me up.

Whack! I squeal.

"What?" he asks coyly. "I'm just adding another handprint to the collection."

I curse under my breath.

"That's not very Christian of you," the smartass remarks.

I give him the finger as I walk out of the shed. I hear his hyena laugh while I'm walking.

When I step inside the clubhouse, Grace is cleaning up the table near the stairs. I'm surprised. From what I've seen, the house is a mess most of the time. With my head down, I try to dart by her. But as I pass her, there's a pull on my arm and I'm yanked back.

"Is it true?" she searches my eyes. "Are you and Axle together?"

I pull my arm out of her grip and take a moment to observe her. There's a slight tug at the corner of her lips, like she's smothering a smile. I don't like it, but I answer her. "Yes."

She shakes her head at me. "Are you really that clueless?" She giggles while my stomach churns. "You think it's a coincidence you're with him? Like you're going to reform a player. People like him don't change."

I peer at Cash, who's joined us. "What are you two talking about?" he asks. His eyes harden when he looks at Grace.

"Nothing," she hastily responds.

He clicks his tongue. "It doesn't look like nothing."

She clears her throat, her eyes darting around. "I better get back to cleaning." Then she leaves.

Cash's eyes search mine. "I don't know what she said to you, but for what it's worth, I've never seen Axle as happy as he is with you."

I smile up at him. "Thank you."

"Is that grease?" He laughs when I reluctantly nod. "I can't take you seriously with the grease on your face. Come into the kitchen. I'm sure we have something that'll help you get it off."

Once Cash has helped me remove the grease, I have a long shower and get into Axle's bed with one of my favorite books. My mind wanders back to Grace, but I put it down to jealousy. I berate myself for even thinking about it because it only puts me in a bad mood. I refuse to lower myself to her level.

I glance at my phone and sigh deeply. My parents haven't reached out to me, and the weight of their silence hangs over me. Yet when I'm with Axle, a comforting presence fills the void, making me feel less alone.

I focus on my romance novel, and soon I'm immersed in the story and thoroughly enjoying my time relaxing while I wait for Axle.

FOURTEEN

I'VE CORRUPTED HER

Axle

"How are you doing with the bikes?"

I look up to see Viper. I stand, reach for a cloth, and wipe my hands. "Good for tomorrow's run. No major repairs and nothing out of the ordinary."

He peers around the shed. "You and Elena are getting close. Has she said she loves you yet?"

My body vibrates with tension, but I plaster on a smile. "Not yet . . ." I answer, but for once, I don't want to talk about it.

His unwavering stare drills holes in me. "You like her," he says. A knowing smirk plays at the corner of his lips.

I frown. I don't know how I feel, so I'm not saying shit.

He mashes his lips together. "Okay, I'll drop it! Tomorrow, what will you say to her about where we're going?"

I shrug. "Just that the club has business to take care of."

"And when she asks what that is?" he probes.

"She's curious about the MC, but I don't think she's ready to know what we do, and that's fine."

"Are you dropping her off at home before we ride out?"

"No!" My answer is fast and sharp. My fists clench at the thought of her roommates' boyfriends and her boss. "Fuck, man, what's with all the questions?"

He gives me a funny look. "So you're going to leave Elena here . . . at the clubhouse . . . with the sweet butts and Twitch."

My head falls back. Not a great idea either. Twitch will be fine, but he's not one to get involved in girl drama if Elena needs help, and I don't trust the sweet butts to not tell her about the bet. "When's the prospect start?" I ask.

"Reaper said he's ready to start whenever. Cash said his War Brothers cut came in yesterday. We can organize a church meeting to discuss it."

I nod. "Let's get it done now. Rage can start before we leave, and his first job can be to watch over Elena."

Viper lets out a small chuckle. "You mean stalk her every move."

"Sounds about right." I need Rage to watch her here at the clubhouse and at her job and at her home. "If something had to happen and I wasn't there, at least Rage would be there, and he can fight."

Viper chuckles. "Elena's not going to like that."

"I don't care." If I didn't make that bet and she didn't work for a creep, I wouldn't have to go to these lengths . . . or would I have anyway? I seem to be a jealous psycho where she's involved. If I don't have to worry about all the bullshit drama because Rage is by her side, I won't have any distractions while riding.

"You go rally the troops. Meet you in church," I say, wanting to check up on Elena first.

He nods, and we head into the clubhouse.

When I reach the door of my bedroom, I peek inside. She's reading a book with a couple kissing on the front cover. I don't know how she has the patience to read. I can't sit still for that long! Not to mention that it would take me years to get through it. Her long blond hair curtains her face. I take a step further . . . Is that . . .? "Fuuuck, babe," I say, and groan. "You look sexy as hell with those glasses on. You're giving me naughty librarian vibes."

She peers up and smiles sweetly.

I make my way to the bed with furrowed brows. "How are you holding up? Sorry for being late; servicing the bikes took longer than I expected." I feel a pang of guilt as I realize she's been waiting for hours. It's strange, this guilt emotion. Can't say I've felt it often.

She slides the bookmark into the book and puts the book down beside her. "It's been a relaxing day. I needed it after all the working I've been doing."

"Good . . . good." I glance down at her book on the bed, then lean over and snatch it. She lunges at me, and I'm eating that shit up. I step away and open the book at the bookmark.

"Give it back!" she snaps, scrambling to get out of bed.

I squint at the black text on the light, creamy page. "When his tongue swirled around my core, I screamed." I chuckle, half turned on and half curious.

Elena is out of bed, jumping at the book, so I raise it higher above my head, to where those little hands can't reach. "Axle!" she yells.

I read another random line. "He kept up a slow, steady rhythm that was pushing me to climax." I laugh while Elena pulls at my arms. "I closed my eyes and burst apart," I say dramatically. "A wave of bliss washed over me." I bring the book down to her, where she grabs it from me with a bright red face. She gets embarrassed so easily. *I fucking love it.* "Here

I was thinking I got an innocent Christian girl, but she kisses like the devil and reads porn."

She scoffs, giving me the evil eye, but I can tell she's trying her best not to smirk at me.

"I've got church now, but I'll be back up soon." I walk back to the door, but I can't stop myself from peering over my shoulder, which is not a good idea. She looks so inviting on my bed. I got lucky with her. I grab my dick through my jeans and playfully narrow my eyes at the sexy vixen. "How am I supposed to go to church with a hard-on?"

She blinks. Her eyes go to my dick, then she licks her damn lips. I growl. She's not helping. I uncomfortably make my way out of the room and down the stairs. I deserve a gold medal for how long I've waited to have sex with her. Seems I won't have to wait much longer, thank fuck! I still can't get over that damn book. I should have known it was porn.

After putting my cell phone in the bowl outside, I walk into church, where everyone's seated around the table, with Reaper at the head. I close the heavy door to ensure club privacy and take my seat on the right, between Viper and Cash.

"Who organized this meeting?" Reaper asks.

"Me," I reply. "Since we have the prospect's cut, can he start like . . . today?"

"Why today?" Bomber asks, his face serious. It won't kill him to smile every now and again. Cranky bastard.

"Because I'd like another guy here to protect the women when we're gone. Give Twitch a chance to focus on the product. It's a good test to see if the prospect is serious about the job."

Demon snorts. "Since when do you give a shit about the women?"

"Since he's in love," Viper says mockingly.

Dickhead! "I am not," I declare, then shove him. He flashes a smirk. "Just shut up," I cut in before the asshole has something else smart to say.

"All in favor of the prospect starting today?" Reaper asks.

I raise my hand, along with everyone else at the table. I let out a shallow breath. That worked out well for me.

"He starts today then," says Reaper. He looks to his right. "Viper, can you call Rage?" Then to his left. "When he arrives, I'll introduce him to everyone, but Bomber, I'd like for you to tell Rage the bylaws of the club and what's expected of him in his role as a prospect."

Reaper looks around the table. "Anyone else have anything to discuss here?" There are subtle head shakes all around, so Reaper bangs the gavel to signal the end of the meeting.

As we walk out, I put my phone back in my pocket and, with a smile, walk back up the stairs to my woman. In my bedroom I grab a clean shirt and jeans from my wardrobe and say, "I'm having a shower, babe."

The hot water soothes my shoulders, which are tense from leaning over the bikes. I roughly dry my body, put on cologne, get dressed, and head back to the room.

I pause when I see the bedroom door is closed. That's weird. When I open it, I drop my clothes on the floor, the same time my jaw hits it. My eyes bulge and all the blood rushes to my dick.

Her shirt is lying discarded on the floor. The blanket just covers her nipples, leaving her creamy skin on display. The only thing around her neck is the gold necklace with the cross on it. She's not even naked and I'm drawn to her. I've never felt this type of powerful pull to a woman before . . . like if I don't touch her or taste her soon, I might die.

I gulp and peel my shirt off my body and throw it on the floor. My heart pounds faster with every step I take toward her. Her chest rises and falls heavily. She looks so angelic, so innocent, but I know better. I crawl into bed. With other women, I just wanted to have sex and get off, or get my dick sucked, but not with her. I want to savor every moment and fuck her so good that she'll never forget about me.

"Lay down, beautiful," I murmur thickly. I'm panting with anticipation as she shuffles down, her big blue eyes resting on me. "I'm dying to fuck you."

She bobs her head, biting her lip. She looks nervous. I kiss the bruise left by the bike falling on her. I clutch the blanket and pull it away from her, gradually lowering it to expose her perfect skin, delicious curves, and perky breasts. I want to burn her body into my memory. I don't know if this will be the only time I see it.

She's still wearing panties, but that's all. When my eyes reach hers again, she's avoiding my gaze. "Hey," I say and cup her chin to lift her eyes to mine. "You're gorgeous . . . you know that?"

Her lips tip up. I kick my jeans off, and her eyes latch on to my dick, making it throb painfully. I lean over, grab a condom, and put it down near her. I grip the thin straps of her underwear and tug. She lifts her hips, granting my request, and I drag her panties down her luscious legs.

I need her mouth. My lips meet hers before I pepper kisses down her neck, along her collarbone to the top of her breast. She squirms, making me grin. My lips close over her pebbled nipple, and her sweet little moan is the best sound I've ever heard. My mouth is watering for more. I don't think I'll ever get enough of her.

Her fingers thread through my hair as I kiss between her breasts, then down her flat stomach. I'm enjoying exploring her body. My hand traces her hip, then I press a soft kiss there. She rubs her thighs together, and I can't stop the cocky grin on my face, knowing she's aching for me.

"We can go as slow as you want," I murmur. I'm drunk,

overcome with need, but I'm holding myself back for her, giving her what she needs.

"I want you to kiss me," she says breathlessly. I crawl up her body. Her arms go around my shoulders and I press my lips to hers. My tongue slips through her parted lips, sending scorching heat through my body. Our tongues move together in a sweet rhythm. When she sucks on my tongue, I let out a low moan.

My fingers work their way down and into her pussy. She's soaking wet. This time I put my fingers to my mouth, tasting her. She licks her lips. My hand goes back down, and this time I push a finger inside, which makes her back bow.

"Oh God . . ." she mutters through heavy breaths.

"Not God, just me, baby."

Two fingers work inside of her now, then my thumb presses on her sweet spot and she bucks. With a swift motion, I reach over, snatch the condom, rip open the packaging using my teeth, and effortlessly roll it onto my erection. I rise over her and her legs open wide for me. I move between her thighs and rest the bulk of my weight on my elbows.

With our bodies pressed together, our lips meet again. The hunger in our kisses is intense. I grab my cock, align it to her, then slowly push it in. She sucks in a harsh breath. "I've got you," I say reassuringly, allowing her to stretch, then slowly rocking in and out of her until her body relaxes.

I slip my hand under her and cup her ass cheek, pulling her against me so that I can go deeper inside of her. I moan aloud; she's hot, wet, tight—perfect. Her fingers dig into my shoulders, and I take that as a sign to speed up. I lick the sweat from her neck.

Our bodies move slickly together. She's throbbing around me. *So fuckin' good.* I drive into her again and again, her cries getting louder. Her fingernails claw my back. Our movements become faster, deeper, harder. She thrashes underneath me.

I'm lost in the moment as her walls constrict around me and she screams. I let out a guttural groan as I follow her over the edge and release into her.

Our breathing is heavy as I drop my face into the crook of her neck. I give us a moment before I pull out, get up, and get rid of the condom in the trash can. When I turn to face her, I nearly step back. Her messy blond hair surrounds her face, her heavy breathing makes her chest rise and fall, and her lips are plump. She tenses when she sees me looking at her and leans down to grab the blanket. I sit on the bed beside her. "Don't be embarrassed, babe. I fucking love your body. You're a dream." I've never been good with words, but I know I could never explain to her how beautiful she is.

Her eyes soften. I pull the blanket back up and lie down next to her. She shuffles into my side and rests her head on my chest. I soothingly stroke her arm until she falls asleep. I want to wake her up and ravage her body again. The way she looks at me, holds on to me, kisses me. I want to hold on to this feeling forever, holding her tight, enjoying the warmth of her in my arms.

I know she has strong feelings for me and knowing that someone like her likes me has made me so happy. Maybe she loves me . . . Wait a second . . . back the fuck up. Do I want her to love me? *I'm not good enough to be loved.* Can I love her? *I don't know.* It's possible what we have is real. Her being here feels right. I close my eyes and drift off to sleep.

I'm woken by a light knock on the door. The room is dark. I yawn. I hear another three knocks, so I gently settle Elena on the bed, shuffle over, then grab my jeans from the floor and get into them, doing up my zipper as I open the door to see Reaper, his face stern.

My guard goes up. "Is everything alright?"

"We've got to do the trip tonight. Everything should stay

the same. The police will stay out of our way, and the Kings of Chaos are meeting us by the Crown Hotel."

I peer over my shoulder at Elena. Damn, I really don't want to leave her. "Is Rage here?"

He gives me a sharp nod. "He's downstairs."

"I'm coming down now." I step inside, grab my shirt, and pull it over my head while I follow Reaper. As I walk downstairs, the men at the bar stare at me. Viper has a smug-ass look on his face. I make my way over to them. "What?"

"Have a good *night*, did you?" asks Viper.

I play stupid, but he knows what happened. I open my mouth, but nothing comes out. I don't want to brag, so I'm unsure what to say.

Viper raises a brow. "Cat got your tongue?"

"How do you know?" I ask.

"The whole MC heard you two having sex. Not exactly quiet," says Cash, smirking.

I ignore their chuckles as I point to Rage and walk to him. His eyes widen, but he stands his ground. "Your first task as prospect is to watch Elena."

"Who's Elena?"

"Short, long blond hair, quiet, absolute stunner. Wears more clothes than the rest of them."

He nods.

"Protect and watch over her at all costs. I mean around the clubhouse, apart from my room. Tell the sweet butts to fuck off if they start any shit. Any mention of a bet—I need you to shut that shit down right away."

"Okay," he answers.

"Oh, there's more. Elena will need to go to work. Take the MC truck. The keys are on the table by the front door. It's important." I put my finger to his chest. "Take her to and from work and sit in the restaurant with her. Keep an eye on her. Her boss is a creep."

He jerks his head in a nod. "Got it."

"I'm not done . . . If Elena wants to go back to her house, follow her inside too. If she wants to sleep there, you sleep on the couch, and you tell her to lock her bedroom door."

"Anything else?" he asks, hiding a smirk.

"Don't be a smartass, prospect." The guy needs to learn his place in the MC. "Yes, there's one more thing." I grab his vest, pulling his head close to mine. "You try to get onto Elena or even look at her the wrong way, I'll chop your dick off and feed it to you." I see the fear in his eyes . . . good. I let go of him. "Well, I won't chop your dick off, but"—I tilt my head in Demon's direction—"he'll do it for me."

Rage's eyes follow mine to Demon, who's playing with his butterfly blade, and then Rage eagerly nods his head. "Understood."

"Hey, Viper," I say with a crooked grin. He turns my way with raised brows. "I think the kid is taking your place as the sexiest club member." The chicks must love this guy.

Viper snorts, but I don't miss him running a hand through his hair.

"Axle." I turn to see Elena, who's now dressed, walking down the stairs toward me. "I woke up and you were gone," she says, frowning sleepily.

I pull her close and kiss the top of her head. "We've got club business on, and we've got to leave tonight."

Her shoulders fall and her body slumps. "Tonight?"

"Yeah, sorry, babe."

She wraps her arms around me, hugging me tightly.

"Time to go," Reaper says, and we all follow him out through the house and out the front door. Everyone's getting on their motorcycles, and engines are roaring to life around me. As I walk to my bike, Elena has a tight grip on me. I chuckle. She's cute.

"Don't leave," she says softly, with pleading eyes.

I turn to her, cup her ass, and lift her until her legs wrap around me and she leans down and presses her lips to mine.

"Come on, lovebirds," Viper yells over the roaring motorcycles.

I set her down on her feet. Sadness shows on her pretty face.

"I've got to go." *Not that I want to.* I could lie in bed with her forever. "Rage, the new prospect, will take you to work."

Elena nods. I lean in, give her one more chaste kiss on the lips, and walk to my bike, start it, and slide my helmet on. There's a gentle touch on my shoulder.

"Be safe," she says, serious now.

"Will do, babe."

Her eyes narrow. "No burnouts!"

I chuckle. "Okay, babe, no burnouts."

It's weird having someone care about me like that, wanting me to be safe, being worried about me . . . it feels good . . . really good. I've never cared about myself, just the club and my brothers. I couldn't care less about my existence.

I reverse my bike and glance back at her one final time, then follow my brothers out of the clubhouse gates.

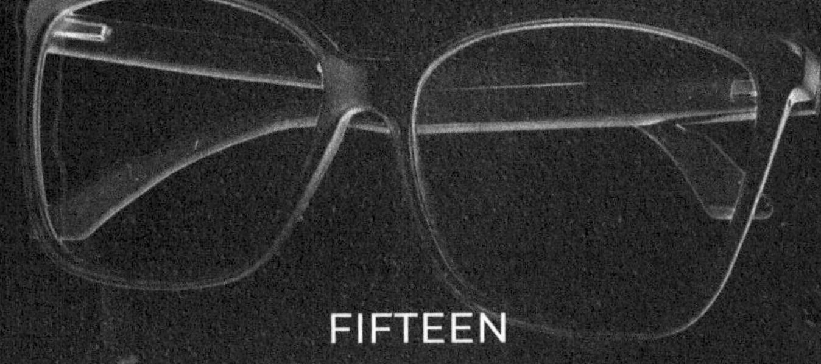

FIFTEEN

HE'S A DRUG AND I CRAVE ANOTHER HIT

Elena

YESTERDAY'S HAPPINESS HAS BEEN DWINDLING SINCE AXLE LEFT. I haven't moved from his bed, although I know I must get ready for work. I grab my phone and message him.

Axle

How is your trip? Did you get there safe? xx

I wait for a reply, but it doesn't come. My stomach churns.

I go downstairs and see the new guy stocking the bar fridges under the watchful eyes of Grace and Mercedez. When he turns, I see the girls weren't wrong—he is very handsome. He's clean-shaven, and I can see the indent of his biceps through his shirt.

"Elena is it?" he asks with a friendly smile.

I smile back. "Yes, and you must be the new prospect."

"The name's Rage." His eyes flick over me, but not in a sleezy way. "Are you ready to leave for work now?"

"I am."

"I'll take you," he says.

I follow him to the front door, but he stops at the computer room. I sense the intensity of Grace's death stare as I wait for him.

"Hey," Rage says to Twitch, who's sitting at his desk. "I'm taking Elena to work. Do you need anything while I'm out?"

"I'm all good, thanks," Twitch replies.

I follow Rage to the shed. The truck beeps, signaling that it's unlocked. I move to the passenger side and stare. With my short legs, how am I supposed to get up?

"Is everything alright?" Rage asks from the back of the truck.

I flush. "Do you mind helping me up?"

He smiles. "Sure." He steps over to me, opens the truck's door like a gentleman, and picks me up like I weigh nothing so that my feet reach the step.

I take a seat and close the door. He gets into the driver's side. As we're driving down the dirt road to town, I glance at him and make small talk. "So . . . why did you want to become a prospect?"

He looks at me for a second before his eyes return to the road. "I got to know the guys through the fights. After school, I never knew what I wanted to do other than fight, so I thought it would be cool to be part of something."

"The women at the clubhouse have taken a liking to you."

"Yes." He chuckles. "They have."

He's been here for only a day, which makes me wonder what the girls have said to him already. "Grace is available."

"Which one's Grace?"

"The one with red hair." Passive-aggressive queen B.

He bops his head. "Thanks for letting me know."

It will make my life easier at the clubhouse if she likes someone else.

Once we get into town, Rage asks, "Where do you work?"

"Crown Village Seafood Restaurant, on the main road."

After he parks outside the restaurant, he comes over to my side of the truck and holds out a hand to help me down. "Thank you," I say, but then I hear the beep of the truck locking. I peer over my shoulder to see Rage following me. "What are you doing?"

He puts his hands in the pockets of his jeans and glances down before making eye contact. "I'm coming with you."

My stomach drops. Of *course he is*. "Axle is forcing you to watch me, isn't he?"

Rage doesn't reply. His lips are set in a firm line. Rage seems harmless, so I decide not to make his life difficult and walk inside.

"She's back," Mel says, her eyes wide. I smile at her, but she looks over my shoulder, her smile brightening ten-fold. She comes over and whispers, "Who's that?"

"Rage. A new prospect for the MC."

"Wow! He's fiiine."

I grin at her and turn to Rage. "Take a seat anywhere. I'll be setting up and assisting in the kitchen."

"I've got to follow you into the kitchen, though."

I blow out a calming breath. "You're literally going to follow me into the kitchen?" I ask, unable to keep the disbelief out of my voice.

"Yes, I can't see you from out here."

He's taking his job too literally. "Trust me, I'll be fine. Axle never followed me in there." Well . . . he did once, but I won't tell Rage that.

Rage gives me a suspicious look.

"Go sit down. You'll find a menu on the table, and you can order something to eat. Would you like a drink?"

"Water, thanks."

I leave, go into the kitchen, and get my apron out.

Mel's at my side. "He's like . . ." She flaps a hand in front of her face, fanning herself.

Cameron comes out of his office with his hands up. "Is that another War Brothers MC member?" He looks me up and down with a sneer. "How many are you with?"

I scoff. Even though I try not to let it, his words still cut. "Axle's got something on, so Rage has decided to . . . join me today."

Cameron straightens his spine. "I told you I don't want any MC members here. You've disappointed me," he says, shaking his head. "If my parents see the security cameras and see you've brought them here, I can't stop them from letting you go."

If I can get another job, I don't really mind, apart from missing out on the good tips. There'd be less bickering between Axle and me.

"Don't you think it's too much?" he asks, but before I can answer, he carries on talking. "It's harassment, and it's not healthy."

"It's not harassment," I'm quick to point out. Unhealthy, maybe . . .

"Oh, they can harass me," Mel says in a sultry voice. I try not to smile at her. Cameron's eyes narrow.

"What? If anything, you'll get more female customers. The cougars with their ugly rich old husbands are going to enjoy perving on him while eating their meals. In saying that, I'm going to go talk to Rage and work my magic." She hastily leaves, and I'm left with Cameron, who's staring at me.

"Your roommates have been asking about you. You should spend some time with them."

I think they only want to talk about or see Axle, not spend

time with me. I don't know how to respond. "I'm busy," is all that comes to mind.

He steps toward me and lifts his hand, but I step back in time before he touches my hair. It seems too personal. Having to be hypervigilant of my boss's actions every time I'm at work is a sickening feeling.

"You're beautiful and deserve so much better than the likes of a club member can offer you."

He just crossed a line! I force my face to be passive because I don't want to cause a scene, especially since Rage can walk in at any moment and I haven't found another job yet.

"Umm . . . I'd better get to work." I briskly walk out and busy myself with work. Time passes and I'm lost, just going through the motions. Menacing thoughts filter through my brain. *Is Axle safe? What's he doing?* Do I want to know? As long as he's safe, that's what really matters.

Mel stops at Rage's table as much as she can. He always smiles at her. She's loving it.

"Where's Axle?" Mel asks when she reaches me.

I frown. I miss him. "He's out with the MC. He'll be back soon."

"Aww . . ."

I raise my eyes to meet hers.

"You really like him."

There's no point denying it. "I do."

The sympathy in her eyes bugs me. "Just be careful. He'll hurt you."

"Thanks." I sigh. "It's not the first time I've heard that."

She lays her hand gently on my arm. "Leopards can't change their spots."

I pull back my arm with more force than necessary and stride toward my bag. "Bye everyone," I call out and go to Rage, who stands.

"Ready?"

"Yes." I follow him to the truck. After being helped inside, I pull out my phone to see messages from two people. Axle and Henry.

Axle

Everything's good babe. We should be back tonight.

Relief floods me.

How's everything been going there? How's Rage?

He's really nice. There was really no need for him to follow me.

Yes. There was. Have you missed me babe?

Yes, I have.

I've missed you too. I've got to go. But I'll see you tonight.

Be safe xx

I gaze through the window of the truck, recalling last night. The way Axle looked at me, like he was starving. Goosebumps travel up my arms. The way he made me feel good and didn't rush me. I appreciate that more than he'll ever know. Everyone portrays him as a player, but he's been attentive, protective, and caring.

I remember that I have a message from Henry.

Henry

I let out an audible sigh. I prefer not to meet him and my parents for my birthday. He's nice, but he's not who I want to spend my birthday with.

"What was that big sigh for?" Rage asks.

"My ex messaged me. My mom has organized for my parents and his family to go out with me for dinner for my birthday."

"Your ex?" he clarifies, looking disturbed.

"Yes."

"Axle doesn't seem the type to let you spend time with your ex. He's very protective of you."

"I've decided I'm not going to go because I want to spend it with Axle instead. I haven't told my parents or my ex yet." I recoil. "My mom will be mad."

"Just tell them. You'll feel better once it's done." He's right.

"I'll do it when we get back to the clubhouse."

Upon our return, I walk through the door and head to the kitchen for water. Vera is pulling the dishes out of the dishwasher while Grace is drying them and putting them away. Mercedez and Candy are seated at the counter.

I give them all a small smile. "Did you screw Rage too?" asks Grace.

I blink at her, taken aback by her words. "I didn't screw him!" I'm offended. "I went to work." *You know, like actual work.* It's on the tip of my tongue, but I keep my cool.

"Well . . . I'm sure Axle won't mind sharing you around," Grace says with a mocking grin.

I scrunch my nose. "He'll care. He gets jealous easily."

Mercedez and Vera are watching us. Candy is looking anywhere but at us, trying not to get involved.

"Why don't *you* spend time with Rage," I say offhandedly, wishing she'd give me a break.

She giggles. "Oh, I will be, but don't get that twisted. I'll be waiting for Axle when you dump him, and you will. It's only a matter of time."

Rage walks in, and his head tilts as he watches me closely. Then it comes to me. Rage is checking on me, making sure I'm alright. I give him a small smile back.

"Hey, Rage," Grace says, trying to sound sexy. She sashays over to him, rubs her hand down his stomach, and then grabs his hand. "Come have a drink with me?"

"Are you alright?" Rage asks me.

"Sure, you go and have a drink." Take her away from me. She's a horrible person.

Grace looks at me, her grin even wider. "Don't forget, whatever happens on a ride, stays on a ride."

I stand and watch Rage and Grace walk to the bar. I'm left wondering what Grace meant by that comment. Vera and Mercedez finish up and leave. Candy remains. "Try not to let them get to you," she mumbles.

"Hmm . . . easier said than done."

"Hopefully, Rage will give Grace someone else to obsess over."

I like Candy. She's always bubbly and positive. "I hope so. What did she mean by whatever happens on a ride stays on a ride?"

Candy cringes. "Well . . . it's a rule with most motorcycle clubs. If the men leave the clubhouse to go to a different town, they can have sex with anyone. So it's not classified as cheating."

Heaviness weighs on my shoulders. I grab my bottle of water and go upstairs to Axle's room. After having sex with me last night, would he have sex with another woman? I'd like to think he wouldn't.

Dread washes over me. I grab my phone from next to the pillow and call my parents.

"Hello," my mother answers.

"Hey, it's me, Elena."

"You have been ignoring us," she says. "No phone calls."

"You know you can call me too." My mouth slams shut. It slipped out before I could stop it.

"What did you say to me?" she asks.

"Nothing," I mumble. "I'm just calling to say I'm not coming home for my birthday."

"You're not what?" she screeches. "Yes, you will. I've organized dinner, made plans with Henry's family. Don't you embarrass me like that! You're coming and that's final."

"Actually . . . I'm not. I appreciate the dinner; send Henry and his family my regards. I've decided I want to have a quiet birthday here."

"You *will* come home!"

"I'm not arguing with you. I told you what I'm doing. See ya, Mom." I disconnect the call and send Henry a message that I won't be seeing him, but I hope he's well.

My phone rings, alternating between my parents' number and his, but I let it ring and lie down, knowing I've got another shift in a couple of hours. I take the time to rest, though my brain won't shut off from the negative thoughts.

Reluctantly, when the time has come, I pull on my uniform, preparing for my next shift. My heart's heavy, and it's hard to shake the unsettling sensation in my stomach. I take a deep breath, forcing a smile that doesn't quite reach my eyes. I'll need to put on a customer service smile tonight.

I go searching for Rage. He's in the living room, Grace on one side, Mercedez on the other. I groan. I'd rather not go to him, but I need a lift.

"Excuse me, Rage. It's time for me to go to work again."

He's on his feet in a second, but the girls whine. I dart out to the truck before I hear what they're saying.

The drive over is silent. He parks outside of work. "Don't you drive?" he asks.

I point over to my sad car that's still sitting there. "That's mine. It's not working."

He chuckles. "Isn't Axle a mechanic?"

"Yes, he is." That reminds me: I need to get onto him about fixing it.

Work goes by slowly, my eyes flickering back to the clock constantly. I'm relieved once my shift is over.

After Rage drives us home, and once I'm out of the truck, I say, "Do you know when Axle will be back?"

Rage replies, "I think he'll be here within the next hour."

Anticipation bursts through my chest. "Finally!"

He chuckles. "You two seem great together. I hope I can find something like that one day."

Oh . . . he's so sweet.

When we go inside, the sweet butts don't affect me . . . nothing does. I'm glowing and have a bounce in my step. Closer to the time Axle's due to arrive, I stay by the front door and wait. My stomach is doing flips, but adrenaline is firing through my veins. He's a drug, and my body aches for another hit.

As soon as I hear the rumble of motorcycles, I run out the front door and impatiently stand on the porch. As they all pull up, I wait until I see Axle, then I hurry down the steps to him. He gets off his bike and takes his helmet off just in time as I launch myself at him and wrap my legs around his waist. I pepper his face with kisses while he laughs.

His head inches back. "I missed you too, baby girl," he says, then presses his lips firmly against mine.

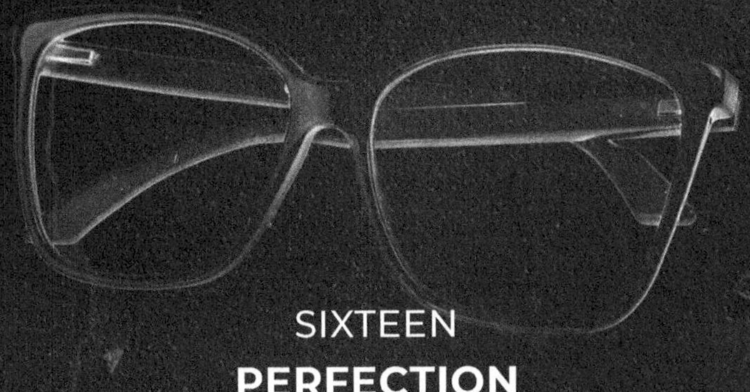

SIXTEEN
PERFECTION

Elena

Lips softly touch mine. My eyelids flutter open to Axle leaning over me.

He inches back. "Happy birthday, babe," he says with a big goofy grin.

I smile back, because how could I not? I know I made the right decision to stay home with him. Axle makes me happy. "Thank you," I reply, my voice still sleepy.

"I'm taking you out to lunch, then I have a surprise for you."

My chest warms and excitement bubbles inside of me. I wonder what it could be. "I've got work today, so we could have breakfast and do everything in the morning."

He shakes his head, smiling mysteriously. "I called your work to say you're having the day off for your birthday. Seriously, who works on their birthday? And you're not having something like ramen noodles or a grilled cheese sandwich for lunch."

I'm a tad annoyed he called my work, but I know he just wants to make today special for me. "A poor person like me still has to work. But I'll enjoy my day off for my birthday with you."

A small frown tugs at the corner of his lips. "I told you I've got money."

"I want to work."

"But . . . you don't have to. I've got heaps of money."

I raise my brow. "Hmm . . . being an MC member earns you a lot of money, does it?"

He averts his gaze, so I put both hands on his cheeks, the way he does to me when he wants me to look at him.

"I have plenty of money because Victor gave me his business when he passed away."

Oh, my heart cracks open for him. "Why don't you run the business if he gave it to you?"

With a subtle shake of his head, he says, "I struggle to read and write. I know nothing about running a business and I'm not a qualified mechanic, so I can't do it. I sold everything but kept his pride and joy—the motorcycle that's in the clubhouse."

I put my arms around him, pull him to me, and hug him tightly. He leans in, and his mouth grazes the side of my neck. He chuckles. "I'm okay . . . It's just difficult to talk about him sometimes." Beneath the cocky exterior, Axle knows pain all too well, but he masks it with quips and an I-don't-care attitude.

He pulls back. "I think you should move in."

I giggle and lightly whack his arm. "Yeah, right."

He smiles wickedly. "You belong in the clubhouse . . . in my bed . . . with me."

I stare at him, waiting for him to laugh or say he's joking, but he doesn't. My heart races. "We haven't been together long enough, and I'm sure you'd get sick of me."

He scoffs. "Get sick of you, baby girl? Never!"

I haven't stayed at home with my roommates for a while now. If I stayed here at the clubhouse, I'd get to see Axle every day. We're like Velcro, spending as much time together as we can. When I'm with him, everything feels right.

"Since it's my birthday . . . how about you inspect my car again," I suggest.

He scrunches his nose. "Nah . . ."

My lips part. "What do you mean, nah?"

He raises his head higher. "I enjoy taking you to work and picking you up."

"I need my car fixed. Please look at it for me." I'm being polite, but my voice holds a warning. He's a mechanic, after all.

Axle rolls his eyes. Cheeky devil. "It's time for your first present."

I tilt my head. "First present?"

He nods slowly, licking his lips, then I feel the heat of his hand between my thighs, making me buck. As his fingers tease my opening, he lowers himself and crushes his mouth to mine, full of all-consuming passion. This is what he does to me. Nothing else matters but us.

His groan vibrates against my lips. "I'll never stop wanting you," he says, and trails kisses down my neck, sparking a fire within me. He slides lower, leaving a trail of kisses until he moves to the middle of my thighs. I can't catch my breath as he places his hands on my legs, opening them wider.

He settles between my thighs, his mouth on me, and I suck in a harsh breath. As he sucks and his tongue dances over my most sensitive spots, I writhe beneath him, one hand curling around the bed sheets, the other tightening my grip on his hair. His stubble only enhances the pleasure.

He sucks on my clit harder and my head sinks into the

pillow. "Oh, Axle," I say through pants. "I can't take it any longer. I want you inside me."

He stops, chuckling. "Damn, babe. Those words coming out of your mouth . . ." He lets out a low whistle, then crawls up my body, his eyes feasting on me. He stops at my necklace. "You know what necklace would look better?"

"What?"

He smirks. "A hand necklace."

"A what—" My words are cut off by his lips colliding with mine. Hard. Demanding. Desperate. I moan beneath his bruising assault.

He pulls back. "Are you on the pill?" he asks.

I can't speak, so I nod. My body burns and my core aches. I want his body pressed against mine. As if he can read my mind, he does just that. My hands slide over his heart. "I love you," I murmur.

He stills, searching my eyes as if trying to determine whether I'm lying.

"Why would you love me?" he asks sadly.

There's a heaviness in my chest at the thought of him not valuing himself. "How could I not love you? You make me feel seen."

His gaze wanders across my face. He looks at me adoringly. "I love you too," he says, and it's the most genuine words I've ever heard him say. I melt into oblivion. I never dreamed of falling in love with a biker, but here I am.

His lips find mine again. He thrusts his tongue into my mouth and kisses me like he needs me like the air he breathes. Desperate for him, I kiss him back just as ruthlessly until his hand goes to his cock. I watch as he pushes himself inside of me. He's so big, but I'm soaked, so he glides into me, even with the tight fit.

His thumb strokes my clit as he sinks to the hilt. He's not gentle this time. Every slam of his hips, every punishing stroke of his cock drives me to orgasm. Over and over, he pounds into me. The rougher he gets, the more turned on I am. Our bodies slap together as he thrusts over and over again.

My muscles tense, my feet curl, and I detonate, screaming in pleasure. I contract around his cock. A moan rips from his chest, echoing through the room. He slams home, pumping his hot cum inside of me. Shaking and pulsing, I ride out the waves. I never imagined I would like sex as rough as that, but with him, I do.

He pulls out and lies beside me, so I shuffle over and rest my head on his chest, listening to the out-of-control beats of his heart. He affectionately presses his lips against the top of my head.

We lie in bed together for hours. I lie in his arms, warm and content.

After we shower, I put on a summery pale-yellow dress. I want to look pretty on my birthday. When we walk downstairs, Cash and Viper are sitting at the bar, talking. They look up at us. "Happy birthday, Elena," Cash says.

My smile is wide as I reply, "Thank you."

Viper leaps off his stool and strolls toward us. When he wraps me in a bear hug, Axle loudly clears his throat. "Happy birthday, darl'," Viper says.

"Thank you."

As Axle and I walk outside hand in hand, I'm elated at the fact that Viper and Cash remembered and said happy birthday to me. I don't recall Henry's friends ever saying it. The men at the MC are different. I'm glad I met them and got to see who they really are.

Axle helps me into the truck, and as I shut the door, I hear Cardi B. My mouth drops open as I shift my gaze from the stereo to him and back again. "I thought you hated my music."

He shrugs and turns it up, making me laugh. When the chorus comes on, he sings it with me. I point to him, my mouth in a perfect O. "You know the lyrics. You're a secret Cardi B fan!"

He scoffs. "I wouldn't go that far." He shrugs. "The song's catchy though."

We drive into town. I smell the salty breeze as it drifts through the window, flicking up my hair. Axle's hand finds mine in my lap, and he gives it a gentle squeeze, a soft smile on his face. He takes me to a café along the main road that I haven't been to before.

The whole time we're there, he's fidgeting with more energy than normal. He seems more excited about my birthday than I am, and it's the sweetest thing.

I take a sip of my cola, appreciating the fine specimen in front of me. Broad shoulders, masculine beard, and the club vest. It's the whole sexy bad boy vibe. An indecent grin is permanently etched on his face, and he makes me laugh every day. Spending time with him is fun.

He's eating his burger, one massive mouthful at a time, and it makes me giggle. I love that he eases my anxiety. I've never had anyone support me like this and remind me not to be taken for granted. Even though we are opposites, we fit and ground one another, encouraging each other to be better people.

My phone rings, distracting me from my thoughts. It's my sister, Ava. "Hello," I answer in a rush, eager to talk to her.

"Hi, Elena, happy birthday!" she says cheerfully.

"Thank you!" I say and smile.

"What are you up to on your birthday? Mom mentioned you weren't having dinner anymore."

The only person I miss not seeing is Ava. "I'm spending my birthday with my boyfriend. We've just had lunch. Now he's got a surprise for me." I peek up at Axle, who has a soft expression on his face.

"I'm so happy to hear you're having a great day. A boyfriend . . . wow, congratulations. We'll have to catch up soon so you can tell me all about him."

"Sounds like a plan," I reply, even though I doubt it will happen because she's so busy now. I make a mental note that if I get married, I mustn't get too caught up with married life and must make time for friends and family. *Not that I have many friends or family members.* I love my sister, and it hurts that we aren't close anymore.

"I miss you," slips out of my mouth, and there's a second of silence.

"I miss you too," she says softly and sincerely. But I wonder, if she shares my feelings, why has she been so distant? All I want is for us to be close again.

Axle twirls his finger in the air, signaling that I should wrap up the call.

"I'll speak to you later. Thanks for calling me." My mood lifts after having talked to Ava. I know she cares about me. She's just busy being a wife now. Maybe I'm just being too needy.

"I don't get it . . . if you miss her, why don't you just talk to her more?"

I shrug. "Ava became distant after she got married. I'm surprised she called for my birthday."

He reaches over and covers my hand with his. "Her loss. Are you finished?" He gives my plate a pointed look.

I laugh. "Yes, I am."

"Second surprise time." Then his face turns serious. "I had no idea what to get you, so I thought I'd take you to one of your favorite places and let you choose what you want."

I smile wide. "Okay, let's go."

He pays, then comes back and takes my hand in his,

kissing the top of it. As we step outside, I walk toward the truck, but he pulls me forward onto the sidewalk. "It's further down there," he says, so I follow him.

We pass a few more restaurants and cross the road. As soon as we reach the corner, I see where we're headed: Crown Village Bookstore. I squeal and bounce on the spot. He laughs, as now I'm pulling him toward the shop. When I open the door, a little bell above it chimes.

"Get as many books as you want," he says with a grin.

I wrap my arms around him tightly. As I pull back, I stand on my toes and kiss him on the cheek. "Thank you, thank you, thank you. This is the best birthday present ever."

His face lights up at my words, and I make my way to the romance section. I pull one book out at a time, check the front cover, turn it around, and read the blurb. I open one of the new releases wide and breathe in the scent of new book, almost getting high on the smell.

When I put the book back, Axle's giving me a weird look. "Don't give me those judgy eyes," I tease him.

He chuckles and shakes his head.

I stack the books in Axle's arms as we go around. I notice the girls around us giggling and checking him out—not that I blame them. If I was in a bookstore and a sexy biker came in and carried around books, I'd be giddy too.

After my shopping spree, a twinge of guilt sets in, but Axle continues to reassure me that it's for my birthday.

When we go back to the clubhouse, we have sex well into the evening. My birthday is perfect.

RIP MY HEART APART

Elena

Yesterday was amazing. I'm excited about reading my books, but I don't know which one to start with. I sit up in bed and read the titles on their spines.

Axle groans. "Lay back down with me." His voice is husky and sleepy.

He tugs on my arm, but I shoo him away. "I want to read one of my books."

He groans again, more dramatically this time, making me chuckle.

"I should have realized giving you books would take your attention away from me."

"Aww . . . poor baby," I coo, trying not to laugh that he's jealous of me reading.

The moment I catch the glint of mischief in his eyes, I brace myself for what's to come. In an instant, he leaps up and gently pushes me back onto the bed. He grips my wrists firmly, pinning them down. I can't help but chuckle, but my laughter quickly fades as his lips meet mine, and suddenly, he becomes my entire world once more.

After breakfast I help the women clean up, even though there's an awkward, silent tension between us. Halfway through, Grace throws the tea towel down on the counter and leans over to whisper something to Vera. How much longer will this continue? Will Grace ever accept that Axle and I are together and just move on? I'll never tell Axle about the way they treat me. I can't expect him to fight all of my battles.

After we finish, Candy turns to me. "Why don't we go watch a movie and let the men do whatever they're doing?"

I nod, giving her a small smile. It's good that Candy seems to be nice and tries to include me, despite the other two being passive-aggressive.

Once we're seated on the couch, Candy grabs the remote and glances at me. "You're very happy today."

Vera comes in and takes a seat on the other side of Candy. I give her a wary stare.

"Absolutely, I am!" I beam. "Axle made my birthday yesterday a very special day."

"Oh. My. God. Happy birthday for yesterday!" Candy says joyfully.

"Thank you."

"So you two are serious then?" she asks curiously.

I nod.

She looks cautiously from me to Vera. "Have you said the *L* word to him yet?"

"What *L* word?" I ask, confused.

"Have you said 'I love you' to him yet?"

Vera's inching toward us to better hear our conversation. "Keep going. I want to know your answer," she says with an evil smile that sends a shiver down my spine. I wonder why they're so interested.

"Yes, we've said it to each other."

Candy gives me a forced smile. "I'm so jealous."

"Does Viper know?" Vera asks me.

I frown. I thought she'd be angry to know that me and Axle are serious, but she's not. I cock my head. "How would I know if Viper knows about me and Axle's discussions?"

"Axle would tell Viper," she says, pouting. "I can guarantee that Viper's not happy about it."

Candy bites her lip and shakes her head at Vera.

My stomach drops. I thought Viper liked me. I wonder why he wouldn't want me and Axle to be together. "What's going on?" I ask, my eyes darting between the two of them.

Raised voices make me turn my head toward the kitchen.

"It's showtime!" Vera says, then looks at me. "Follow me if you want to know what I'm talking about."

Anxiety shoots through me. I should stay exactly where I am if Candy's deep frown is anything to go by. Nothing good could come of what Vera has to say, but I don't like secrets and I want to know what she's referring to.

Vera walks down the hallway and I follow. She's smiling smugly and my stomach is queasy, my heartbeat erratic.

"You know you're not the only one Axle's slept with since he's been talking to you," Vera says in a hushed voice.

I shake my head. I don't believe her, because I don't trust her.

She nonchalantly shrugs. "I just thought you should know . . . because if you love him . . . I know I'd want to know if he was cheating on me."

I yank at the collar of my shirt, which has constricted around my throat. We keep walking until we reach the kitchen. We're behind the wall, so no one else can see us. There's yelling. The voices belong to Grace and Axle. I start to step forward, but Vera grabs my arm and shakes her head.

"I thought she was a bet . . . a joke, but you're the one that looks like a fool because you've fallen for her!" Grace yells.

My body grows cold. My mind spins . . . a bet . . . a joke. *No!* This isn't happening. I grab my heart that's now gaping wide open.

Axle laughs coldly. "You know nothing about how I feel."

Why isn't he calling her a liar?

"Yes, I do," Grace says. "You never looked at me the way you look at her." She's furious, but her voice is tinged with sadness.

"Do you listen to a word I say?" Axle bites back. "I don't know, maybe the one hundredth time I said we were only having sex. Stop your jealousy bullshit and get over it."

"Of course I'm jealous!" she screeches, making me jerk. "I wanted to be your ol' lady."

He scoffs. "Well . . . that was never going to happen. I didn't even know I wanted an ol' lady until Elena."

"Does your Saint Mother Teresa know about the bet with Viper yet?"

I assume I'm the Mother Teresa she's referring to.

"If you dare say a word to Elena . . ." His voice is threatening.

Bet . . . A wave of nausea hits me. I fight back the urge to vomit. Tears fall fast, wetting my cheeks, but I don't wipe away these tears of pain.

"Congratulations," Grace says in a sickly-sweet tone. "You won the bet—you made her fall in love with you."

And with that the knife goes through my heart and I can feel the jagged end slice right through me.

She giggles loudly. "Have you collected your money from Viper yet?"

And the knife continues pushing through my back. I clasp my hands over my mouth, trying to stop the sobbing.

"That's enough!" Axle shouts.

"I don't want to break her little heart," she mocks. "But I

can tell you right now she's going to find out. Secrets don't stay hidden."

"Yes, they can," Axle says harshly.

A cry tears from my mouth. I can't stop it. My chest burns. It's like I'm underwater and trying to breathe. I turn the corner. Grace and Axle look up, startled.

Grace's smile is triumphant. She clicks her tongue. "Oops . . . looks like she knows now!"

Axle's hands go to his head. "Elena . . ." He looks distraught, but I don't believe it. He grabs at the base of his throat. "Let me explain," he says, taking a cautious step toward me.

"All this time you were pretending . . .?" I ask, my voice breaking at the end. "How could I have been so stupid?"

He takes another step, but I move back. "Don't come near me," I cry out through sniffles and a flood of tears.

"That bet was only at the beginning . . ." he says in a rush of words. "Then I met you, spent time with you . . . and it all changed for me." His eyes are glassy and he sounds sincere, but all I hear is more lies. Being with him was an illusion. He's exactly the person everyone warned me about.

"I don't believe you!" I yell at him with disgust. "I trusted you . . . I loved you . . . How could you?" My voice softens at the end, laying bare the excruciating, raw pain within me.

I turn and leave. I can't even look at him. I run through the house, past people staring at me with open curiosity, with Axle's heavy footsteps behind me. He grabs my arm. I yank it back. "Don't *ever* touch me again." My voice reverberates through the space, tinged with hurt but also rippling with anger.

"I'm sorry . . ." He tugs at his hair. "It was before I got to know you . . . You have to believe me."

I pause to meet his pained gaze. "I've got no reason to

believe anything you say anymore." I wipe the tears from my eyes, but it's no use. They keep falling.

He reaches for me again but stops and drops his arm to his side. "I'm sorry," he says again. "I hate that I did this to you. You mean everything to me. You know you do."

I thought I did. I don't know what to believe anymore. A storm brews within me, where sorrow and rage collide. I keep walking up the stairs and still hear him behind me. "If you've ever had any respect for me at all . . . *don't* follow me," I hiss. I need to escape this place. I'm suffocating.

He stops and I dash upstairs and to his room. I shove my clothes and books into my bag and swing it over my shoulder. Cash is outside Axle's bedroom when I rush out.

"I'll give you a ride home in the truck," he says.

I realize I'm stuck here otherwise. "Thank you," I whisper, appreciative of his kindness. I follow Cash until we meet Axle, who hasn't moved. I refuse to look at him. How could he be so callous?

"I'll get her home safe," Cash says.

I follow Cash down the stairs and we dart outside, where I struggle to draw air into my lungs. My body is as cold as ice, and my heart constricts. It's alarming how effortlessly Axle lied to me. He told me he loved me, wanted me to move in with him . . . Devastation and disbelief bleed out of me with every step to the truck.

EIGHTEEN

WOLF IN SHEEP'S CLOTHING

Elena

Deceit. Betrayal. Pain.

I'm lying in my bed, on my stomach, holding my pillow and looking absently at the wall, when I hear a light knock on my door.

"It's Lucy. I just wanted to check you're okay."

When I arrived home, Lucy, Cindy, and Jasmine were chatting in the living room. Their conversation halted as they saw me bolt upstairs, my face flushed and eyes brimming with tears.

"Of course she's not okay," Cindy says. "I bet Axle dumped her."

I shut my eyes for a moment. Everyone doubted our relationship.

"Shhh! You don't know that," Lucy says.

"Oh, come on. You didn't believe Axle was going to change," Jasmine says arrogantly.

"I'm fine," I say, though the tone of my voice says

otherwise.

"Okay . . . well, I'm here if you need to talk," Lucy says.

I have no desire to. Especially to Jasmine, who will give me the I-told-you-so speech. And I would rather avoid seeing the sympathy in their eyes. I'm pathetic. Someone gives me an ounce of attention and I'm hooked. I give them everything, to my detriment.

I roughly rub my tears away. I shouldn't have gotten involved with Axle. His presence tricked me into thinking I meant more to him, but everything was fake. I was just a victim of his manipulation. He worked me like a puppet and showed no mercy. Axle said he loved me. He's nothing but a wolf in sheep's clothing.

My phone rings again, but I let it ring out because I know who it'll be. Axle ripped my heart out. Now he's got blood on his hands. I can't bring myself to talk to him. Not now . . . not today, possibly never. He's just going to say all the right things like he usually does.

Perhaps Axle's hazel eyes, crooked smile, and easy charm were what put me at ease and made me lower my guard. He said I trust too easily. I thought I knew him. I never imagined him to be so heartless. Vera said there were other girls . . . how many? I feel so stupid. Everyone warned me about him. I guess some people don't change.

I snuggle into my pillow and close my eyes, taking deep breaths. I need sleep to take the pain away because I need peace, and moments later, I finally get it.

My eyes open to the buzzing of my phone and the bright light of its screen. It's dark outside. I check my phone and see eight missed calls from Axle. It's getting late—it's eight thirty. Mouth dry, I rise and drag myself to the door. I take a second to get myself together to face my roommates before I open the door and go downstairs.

I had hoped they'd all be in bed, but voices are coming from the living room.

"Elena," Lucy calls out. I pause and slowly pivot to see them sitting on the couches. Then I spot my boss with them. *Could it get any worse?* I fake a smile, then turn and go to the fridge to get a bottle of water. I don't even get a sip down before Lucy and Jasmine are standing directly in front of me.

"What happened?" Lucy asks in a small voice.

"It's Axle, isn't it? I told you he'd break your heart," Jasmine says in the same tone Grace used. "He slept with me, then ignored me like I never existed. Don't take it personally —it's just who he is."

Don't cry. Don't cry. I clear my throat. "We broke up." Lucy places her palm on my arm. "I'm going to go back to sleep," I tell them. "Have a good night, you two."

As I walk away and reach the bottom of the stairs, Cameron calls my name, making me halt and internally groan as he walks over.

"Is everything alright?" he asks.

I nod. "I'll be okay." I try to sound like I'm fine, but I'm not and I don't know if I ever will be. Cameron puts his arms around me and hugs me tightly. I cringe, feeling uneasy, but to not make it even more awkward, I pat his back with one hand.

He pulls back with a smile. "If it's about the biker, I've always known you could do better. You don't want to get yourself mixed up with those types of people."

"Those types of people" make me narrow my eyes. He has no idea what the MC stands for and who they are. Axle might have broken my heart, but I refuse to listen to people badmouth the MC because I know they are good men. I pull myself out of his hold. "You don't know them. They served our country in the military and are a friendly bunch of people. I have no idea why you think so poorly of them, but I'd appreciate it if you said nothing negative in my presence."

His eyes widen. The silence is loud. He rubs the back of his neck. "Sorry."

No, he's not. I look at the stairs. "I'm going to bed."

"Are you coming to work tomorrow?" he asks.

Just the thought has me cringing. "Sure, I'll be there tomorrow." I've had time off. I can't afford to give up another shift.

"Both shifts?"

At least it will keep my mind busy. "Yes," I reply. "Good night." I dash up the stairs before he keeps talking to me. My shoulders are heavy and my chest aches. I don't feel like discussing it with anyone, so tomorrow is going to be hell with Mel. I go into my room, then change into my pajamas.

After I lie down, I grip my phone. My thumb hovers over the notifications. I don't think I could talk to Axle now, but I do want to read the messages. *No!* I force myself to turn the vibration and sound off before turning my phone upside down, the screen facing the nightstand. I drift off to sleep.

From the moment I wake up, I see Axle's face. I swallow forcefully and rub my chest, recalling Grace's words. Axle warned me he's poison. I should have listened. I so easily ignored the red flags that kept popping up with everyone warning me about him.

After I shower, I change into my work clothes. I feel slightly better from the hot water and the fact that it hid the tears that silently flowed. I walk down the stairs and bolt out the door, trying to avoid my roommates. When I step onto the porch, I freeze. The War Brothers MC truck is outside, with Cash behind the wheel.

Of course. My car hasn't been fixed. My head falls back. How am I going to get to and from work every day? I stroll to the truck. "Thank you for picking me up. You didn't have to."

He grins, though the sympathy in his eyes is unmistakable. "Yes, I did. Axle's working on your car now."

My stomach plummets. "He's fixing my car now? Out the front of my work?"

"Yes," he replies.

"I would rather not see him." I blink furiously, trying not to cry. But I know I need my car fixed and I have to go to work right now.

"Do you still want to go?" Cash asks.

"Yes," I reply with a heavy sigh. I don't want to, but it's not like I have a choice. I stare out the window on the short drive.

Cash parks the truck. Before I get out, I say, "Thanks for the ride." As I'm closing the door, I peer up at my car and see Axle jogging over to me. I turn away from him and quickly walk toward the restaurant until I feel a hand grasping my arm. When I turn to him, I shake my head, glaring at him.

He's clutching me desperately, but his hand then slips away. "Sorry." He's breathing heavily and frowning. He has bags under his eyes, and his hair is sticking up like he's been tugging at it. "I've sent you a bunch of messages."

"I got them, but I haven't read them." I lift my hand in a stopping motion. "I can't do this right now. I've got work." I step to the side, but he does too.

"You need to listen to my side of the story."

Hurt turns to irritation. "Why should I?" I raise my voice. "So I can listen to more lies? Haven't you stolen enough from me?" *My heart . . . my time.* But maybe he needs to hear the pain he's caused. "How could you lie to my face?" I don't let him answer. "You have no respect for me. You just play mind games, and I'm the idiot who fell for it."

His head jerks. "No, I love you," he insists, his voice thick with emotion. "You felt it too, didn't you?" He lowers his voice. It's almost a whisper now as vulnerability washes over his features. "I was never fake with you."

I laugh rudely. I might be losing my mind. "You don't love me. You'd never be able to hurt someone you love the way you've hurt me."

He looks down, then back at me. "I'm sorry I hurt you. I'm an asshole and I fucked everything up, but I made the bet before I met you. Then things changed. I didn't take the money."

I grit my teeth at his words. "Do you want a pat on the back for not taking the money?" I'm burning up as anger pours out of me.

He raises his hands defensively. "No."

I see Mel and Cameron standing by the front door of the restaurant. I need to just walk away, but I can't help myself and ask, "What about the other girls then? How many were there?"

He frowns and cocks his head to the side. "What other girls? What are you talking about?"

"Vera said you were cheating on me with other girls."

He swears under his breath. "She's a fuckin' liar."

"Seems you two have that in common."

He paces. "I was never with anyone while I was with you. The last time I was with a chick was literally the night we spoke on the phone for the first time. That was it! And anyway, you were the one talking to your ex."

Rage told him. "We have only texted. At least I don't *live* with my ex," I bite back. I hate that I'm yelling at him, but at least I'm standing up for myself.

Mel walks toward us. "I'm coming," I say to her and brush past Axle.

"I love you, and I'm not just going to let you walk away from what we have."

I stare up at his handsome face. My vision blurs. "You can't fix us . . ." I whisper and walk to Mel.

I dart inside the restaurant with Mel close behind. I rush into the bathroom and go to the basin to wet my burning face. At least Axle looks like he's in pain, so there might be a part of him that's upset too. But is he upset because he got caught out or is he truly upset about what he did to me? Now I'm questioning everything.

Mel rests her hand on my back. "What happened?"

I rub under my eyes and clear my throat. "We broke up."

"Oh no." Her voice sounds sympathetic, but the smile tugging at the corner of her mouth reveals that her true emotions are quite different. She reminds me of Grace and Vera.

"I'm fine," I say before she says anything else. "We'd better get to work." I square my shoulders and plaster on a fake smile—fake it till you make it. But Axle's words haunt me as I work. I do my best to keep my distance from Mel and Cameron, but at the end of my shift Cameron calls me over.

When I reach him, I say, "I'm sorry I dropped the plates." Luckily, there were only two and they just had leftover food on them.

"No need to apologize." He tucks a stray strand of hair behind my ear.

My muscles tense and my heart accelerates. He drops his hand to my shoulder and rubs my arm. I'm so mentally exhausted I can't bring myself to say how uncomfortable he's making me.

"You should come have a few drinks with me after work one day. Loosen up and forget about everything."

To forget and not experience pain sounds appealing. I muster up all my energy and give him a small smile. "I'll think about it."

Once my shift finishes, I grab my bag. Mel is by my side.

"What happened? Did he break up with you?" she asks.

"I don't want to talk about it." The shortness of my reply should signal that I mean it, but she keeps going.

"Why won't you talk to me about it?" she asks, sounding irritated.

I stare at her dumbfounded. The nerve of her. How is she making this about her? "It's none of your business," I say sternly. I'm sick of people manipulating me and being fake.

Her mouth slams shut and her eyes widen.

I ignore her and peek out the front door. The MC truck is waiting outside, in the closest parking space. Mel walks past me, straight to the driver's side. Annoyance flares. What if it's Axle? Would she go there even though we broke up yesterday? I don't trust her, so I swiftly walk to the truck. When I open the door, Viper smiles at me.

"Nice to meet you," he says to Mel.

"You too," she says, batting her eyelashes.

I snort. Viper puts the car in drive, and we pull out. My eyes are on my car as we go.

"Axle said it is working fine now, so you can drive it home after your shift tonight," Viper says, like he knows what I'm thinking.

"Hmmm . . . I bet he's the one who broke my car."

No response. I whip around to glare at Viper. When Axle learned about the sexual assault claim against my boss, my car *suddenly* stopped working. "I can't believe him!" I hiss.

Viper chuckles.

My eyes narrow. "It isn't funny!"

He shrugs. "It's his way of trying to protect you."

"Protect me?" I huff. "You mean manipulate me?"

When we pull up outside my house, Viper turns to me. "He really loves you."

I roll my eyes. I don't think any of the men would know what love is if it hit them in the face.

"I never thought any of us would have an ol' lady, let alone Axle. But I've never seen him so torn up. It was my fault too. I shouldn't have been a dick and goaded him, but after he spent time with you, whenever I mentioned the bet to him, he always got defensive and was short with me."

The fight within me dwindles, leaving only a deep sense of exhaustion. I release a long, weary sigh. "It's not your fault," I whisper, though the words feel heavy as sorrow threatens to engulf me entirely. "He broke me, Viper, and it hurts all the way to my soul, knowing I can't trust him or be around him anymore." Pain tinges every word as my tears fall.

Viper leans over, puts his arm around me, rubs my back. I'm grateful for his compassion.

NINETEEN
WAR OF GUILT

Axle

I'VE ASKED VIPER TO TELL ELENA HER CAR IS FIXED, BECAUSE I know she won't answer my call. I sense the stares of the other men as I walk straight to the bar, grab a full bottle of whiskey, twist off the cap, and take a gulp. The burn of the liquor matches my burning rage. I do it once more, then sit down. "Can you grab me a beer?" I ask Rage, who's behind the bar, giving me a cautious look.

"Uh, sure," he says. He grabs a beer for me and puts it in front of me.

I take a swig, craving the numbness brought by alcohol. I rub my eye and wonder how everything got so fucked up. I had one fucking job . . . one job . . . win the bet . . . don't make it personal. Noooo, not greedy me. I'm always searching for the next high, so I gave in to temptation. I had to fucking taste her . . . then I was a goner. I messed up one of the best things in my life. I chuckle. I'm good at fucking things up . . . no, I'm a master of fucking things up. All we had is gone, and I'm the one to blame.

After ten beers, the pain has lessened but I still feel like shit. Memories of the pain in Elena's eyes and the sob. I groan. That fucking sound of her crying. It guts me. And to think I did that to her? I cracked her smile . . . I was the one who broke her.

The men are talking around me, but I hear nothing they say. I stare off into space, thinking about Elena. Those seductive eyes, that rockin' body . . . She was nice to me—not that I deserved it. It's hard to find someone as genuine as she is. She's rare. She didn't care about the cut; she wanted to get to know me . . . and no woman has cared to get to know me before.

I peer down at my phone, press the home button. No messages or phone calls. What did I expect?

Viper sits down next to me and slaps me on the back. "I hate seeing you like this, brother. I thought I'd let you know I spoke to her."

"What did she say?" I inch toward him, hanging on his every word.

"She was crying, and I could tell she misses you. Tell her how you feel, then give her time to process it."

This was coming from the biggest player of us all.

"I tried to explain everything to her the other day when Cash dropped her off. I told her we made the bet before I met her. Everything changed afterwards. Vera said I was having sex with other women." I pause, then mutter, "Bitch," under my breath. "I was exclusive with Elena, and it still somehow gets thrown in my face that I was cheating."

"As I said . . . give her some space," he says.

Not possible. "You know me. How am I going to give Elena space?" My mouth twists at the idea. "She needs reminding every fucking day that she belongs with me and that I want her back."

Viper shakes his head. "It's not about you, it's about her. At least give her a few days."

I grab my phone, then stand and shove it into my jeans pocket, knowing not talking to Elena is going to be torture. We've grown so close. I bring the bottle to my lips and drain the remainder of the beer. "I'm going to lie down for a bit."

He nods. "Take it easy, man."

I stumble through the clubhouse, aware of the men's penetrating stares. Hanging on to the handrail, I climb the stairs, make it to my bedroom, and collapse onto my bed. Elena's scent on the pillow is like a punch to the face. Fuck, I miss her. I don't know how I'm going to last even a few days without her.

I WAKE, GASPING FOR AIR. I'M DRENCHED IN A COLD SWEAT. I reach out, desperately searching the bed for Elena, but she's not there. Reality is brutal. I see her shadow everywhere I go, even in the dark, but I'm alone. I've never understood the true meaning of relationships until I met Elena.

Three whole days I've waited. I find comfort in alcohol, sleep off the hangover, then eat and sulk. Going from my bedroom to the bar and back again. Cash, Viper, and Reaper have tried to talk to me, in whatever way they can, but nothing helps the crushing guilt that weighs heavy on my chest, every goddamn day. I roll over and stare at where Elena used to lie. I don't know how much longer I can take this.

Back in the bar, I'm swirling beer around in my glass, watching as it slides around. I hear women talking and shift my gaze to Vera and Grace. Their eyes widen when they see me, and they hightail it out of here. They've been avoiding me, which is a smart move on their behalf, because I just want to let loose on them for destroying the best thing in my life.

Every day the tension in me rises. I feel it in my shoulders. The anger gets worse daily. I fist my hand tightly. I'm going to snap soon. I can feel it.

I roll my head back. My neck cracks. *Fuck this!* I stumble through the clubhouse and grab my bike key off the table. As I walk toward the front door, I hear, "You're not fucking riding like that. You're wasted."

I turn at the sound of Reaper's voice. I respect Reaper, but for the first time, I don't want to abide by his rules.

"Rage," Reaper calls out, "can you take Axle wherever he wants to go?"

"Sure thing," Rage answers and walks toward us. "Where are we going?" he asks as we walk outside.

"Elena's house. I'll give you directions."

His eyes widen, but he keeps his mouth shut.

When we arrive, I say, "Park behind that car." I point to Elena's car. At least it's running now, so she doesn't have to rely on anyone for a lift to and from work.

My heart's slamming against my ribs, and just for a second I wonder if I'm doing the right thing. *Does she hate me?* I clench my fists again. I need to pull myself together. I take a moment, sitting in the car in silence, before I get out and walk toward the house.

I open the front door and walk inside. Four girls are staring at me from the couch. "Where's Elena?" I point to the stairs. "Is she in her room?"

The black-haired one jumps up, rushes over, and stands between me and the staircase. I have to woosah myself to calm the fuck down. "What are you doing?" I snap. "Let me through."

She jerks, but then smiles smugly at me. Maybe this is karma for sleeping with heaps of women.

"Elena doesn't want to see you."

The self-satisfaction in her voice irritates me further. "Let me be the judge of that."

She pouts. "No. She wants to be left alone."

"Who are you to say anything?" I chuckle darkly. "You hardly even know Elena, let alone are friends with her. What . . . I fucked you, now you're trying to get back at me?"

The girls in the background let out a gasp. The girl standing in front of me drops her shoulders. Perhaps I shouldn't have lashed out, but she's standing between me and Elena right now.

The blond girl walks over. "Uh, I think it might be best if you leave. I'll tell Elena you were here."

Breathe in . . . breathe out. I storm out of the house, then get into the truck with Rage. "Let's go home. I need another drink."

TWENTY
BROKEN TRUST

Axle

More days pass. No messages, no missed calls. I thought about turning up at Elena's doorstep again or going to her work, but I don't know if it's going to make the situation worse. Every second of every day, I'm haunted by her. I'll never forget the taste of her lips. I remember how my fingertips dragged across her smooth, soft skin, over her curves.

It's Friday night and Viper's organized a clubhouse party. I think he just feels bad for me. Everyone is outside, huddled together, talking in groups, while the music's blasting. I gaze down at my still-full beer. I am not in the mood to drink tonight. My body has had enough.

A girl sits close to me. I glance at her face. She's smiling widely. "I know you," I say, though I can't put my finger on how or where I know her from.

"I work with Elena."

Elena . . . just her name is enough to cause me pain. "How's she doing?" I have to ask.

"Quiet . . . sad. Comes to work and goes straight home." She puts her hand over mine. "And how are you doing?"

I pull away from her, curling my lip. She's fooling herself if she thinks I'd have anything to do with her.

"I wouldn't worry about trying to get back with Elena if I were you."

Here we go . . . "Hmmm . . . and why's that?"

"I'm sure she's getting drunk right now, trying to get over you."

My chest is tight. All senses on high alert. "What did you just say?" I sneer, hoping I heard her wrong, because Elena hardly drinks.

The girl pouts. "They're having a party at their house tonight. I was told it's going to be huge, so I'm sure she'll be finding someone to try to get over you."

She reaches for me, but I shove her hand away. *Elena drunk . . . her boss* . . . "Fuck!" The tension in my voice cuts through the air. I take a few quick steps over to the clubhouse and punch the window. It shatters with a high-pitched crack, shards of glass falling to the ground. My hand aches. Blood drips down but I barely notice.

Demon is closest to me. He walks over and looks at my hand. "What's going on with you? Is everything alright?"

The anger swells inside of me. My body is on fire. "No, I'm not. Come with me?" I pause. "I need to check on Elena, so you might get to have some fun if anyone dares to touch her."

A sardonic grin envelops his face. "I'm in."

I knew he would be. He's twisted. We're both a little unhinged. I'm reckless, but he's higher on the psycho scale than me.

Viper and Cash are watching me closely. Cash stands, but as he walks toward me, I mumble to Demon, "Quick. Let's get out of here before they try to stop us."

Demon gives me a sharp nod. "I'll get the keys. Meet you in the van."

"Get me a tea towel from inside for my hand."

As Demon walks away, I glance at Cash. "I'm alright. Demon's just getting something for my hand."

He gives me a slow nod.

I hurry along the side of the house and to the van. If Elena's boss is there with her . . . if he tries anything . . . My hands ball into fists. I swear I'll kill him.

Elena

THE HOUSE IS FULL OF STRANGERS. SOME DANCING AND OTHERS talking. I cough from the cloud of cigarette smoke.

"I'm so happy you could join us," Lucy says with a wide smile, and then she bumps her hip against mine.

I give her a fake smile in return. I regret agreeing, but after a long week I need this distraction. I just don't want to think about Axle. He's under my skin. It pains me to know I still love him, even with all the heartbreak he's caused me. I don't regret the time spent with him, because he made me happy. No matter how hard I try, I can't hate him.

"Here," Lucy says, handing me another full shot glass. This time there's red liquid in it. She raises hers and we clink our glasses together. "To getting over Axle."

"Cheers," I say and swallow in two gulps. Instantly a sharp burn hits my throat, making me cough and my face twist into a grimace. "Oh, that one's strong." It warms my belly, but my head spins. Someone grips my shoulders, and I turn to see Cameron.

"You need to relax," he says softly, gently working his fingers into my shoulders.

My body stiffens slightly, but I'm too sluggish to move away from him. "I am relaxed," I murmur.

He laughs. "Not relaxed enough. How many shots have you had?" he asks, then looks between me and Lucy.

Lucy shrugs. "We're still standing," she says, then giggles. "Alcohol will help her forget . . . at least for tonight, anyway."

I peer down at the empty shot glass. "Well . . . pour me another."

"That's the spirit," Cameron says.

Cameron pours me another shot and reaches over to pass it to me. I blink a few times. I see two shot glasses, though I'm pretty sure my eyes are playing tricks on me.

Cameron laughs and brings the glass to my lips. I swallow the shot down.

My head falls to the side. Everything's spinning. I grab the kitchen counter to stay upright.

"Are you alright?" Lucy asks, sounding worried.

I rub my forehead. *No, I am not.*

"I'll take her to her bedroom so she can lie down," says Cameron.

Hmm, bed . . . seems like such a good idea right about now.

"Are you sure?" Lucy asks him or me. I'm not exactly sure at this point. I just want to be in my warm, comfortable bed.

"It's fine. I'll get her there safe and tucked in bed," he replies.

Cameron grabs my hips, helping me stand. "Woah . . ." I mutter. We walk around the bunch of bodies. I put my arm over his shoulder as we step up the stairs. He wraps his arm around my waist, pulling me tight against his body. When we reach the top, he wiggles my bedroom doorknob.

"It's locked. Do you have the key?"

My eyes are heavy, but I point to my pocket. He dips his hand into my pocket. It lingers there, and then he rubs the edge of my privates. I take a step back, nearly losing my foot-ing. "What are you doing?" I slur.

He smirks. "Helping you into your room." He unlocks the door and guides me inside and eases me down on my bed. He leans over and brushes my hair out of my face.

"Mm," I grunt. I want to go to sleep.

He leans over me. "I'm going to make you forget that piece of trash. I'm going to make you feel good." His lips crash into mine.

Shock turns my body to stone. *No . . . this can't be happen-ing. I don't want him.* I squirm, trying to pull away, but I'm struggling. His body is heavy. I'm drunk, but I know I don't want this. He grabs my boob roughly.

"Don't," I say, but he doesn't listen. He kisses down my neck while I'm struggling beneath him, my heart racing, my stomach queasy.

"Get off me!" I say, louder. I try to push him off, but he's so strong.

He's frowning. "What, you can take dick from a biker, but you don't want mine?"

I blink at him. Worry clutches at me. *Will he hurt me . . . rape me?*

The door crashes against the wall with a loud thud, jolting Cameron upright. He leaps off me, eyes wide with panic, and hurriedly backs away to the far corner of the room. His voice is shaky as he protests, "It's not what it looks like."

Axle's chilling gaze is aimed at Cameron, the hostility radiating off him. Instant relief eases my heavy heart. *He's here. He will protect me.* Axle darts to Cameron and grabs him by the throat. Cameron's feet are dangling. "I'll fucking bury you!" Axle screams in his face.

Demon kicks the bedroom door closed. His smile is amused, and a wicked glint dances in his eyes. A dull crunch pulls my attention back to Axle. He's out of control, throwing punch after punch at Cameron's face. Demon creeps toward him, his smile curving higher. He pulls Axle off Cameron.

Axle glares at Demon. "Get the fuck off me."

Demon doesn't flinch. "I'll take care of him." He peers at me and his gaze softens. "You tend to her. I'll meet you at the van in ten."

Axle turns to me and his shoulders fall. He takes cautious steps toward me, then takes my shaky hand in his and helps me sit upright. I notice the blood and redness on his hands and knuckles. He scoops me up, one arm supporting my legs and the other my back and pulls me to his chest. His heart is hammering against me, and his breathing is heavy. He kisses the top of my head.

As we walk out, Demon says, "You're mine, motherfucker."

The terrified scream that follows makes me flinch, but I have no sympathy for Cameron because I know he would have tried to rape me if he'd had the chance. Axle closes the bedroom door behind us and carries me down the stairs. His body is stiff, as if violence is still coursing through his veins, but his need to care for me outweighs that part of him.

The screams fade away, drowned out by the blaring music. I burrow deeper into the comforting warmth of Axle's chest, choosing not to meet anyone's gaze. He kisses the top of my head again.

"I'm so sorry," he says just loud enough that I can hear it.

It's not your fault. I want to reassure him, but the words catch in my throat, leaving me unable to speak.

Outside, he opens the van door and ever so gently places me down on the seat. His eyes drift over my face and body. With a pained expression, he asks, "Did he hurt you?"

I shake my head. Physically, no . . . I tug at Axle's shirt, needing him to stay with me. He sits on the seat beside me and pulls me down so that my head is resting on his lap. He strokes my hair and whispers, "I've got you."

Tears well up as I imagine what might have been. Despite Axle using violence against people who hurt me, I feel an undeniable sense of security when I'm wrapped in his arms. His protective presence is unwavering, and I know he'll always be there to keep me safe.

His eyes, full of determination, meet mine, offering a silent promise that reassures me. "Don't cry, baby girl," he says softly as he wipes my falling tears with his thumb. There's a pain in his voice and I want to stop crying, but I can't.

A short while later, the front door slams shut, making me jolt.

"Shhh . . ." Axle says. "It's just Demon."

The van starts and we pull away. "Did you hurt him?" Axle asks menacingly.

Demon lets out a dark chuckle. "Sure did. My knife went through both his hands. He'll think twice before touching another woman against her will. I told him if it happens again, he'll be six feet under."

"Thanks, brother."

"Good times," Demon replies.

TWENTY-ONE
SHE'S MY RIDE OR DIE

Axle

Elena fell asleep in the car, so I carried her to bed and made sure she was asleep before I went to the bathroom to wash the blood off my hands. Adrenaline is still firing through me. I've lost control many times, but never to the point where I wanted to kill someone.

Bomber knocks on the door, his face sterner than normal. "Church, now!"

"Okay," I respond. A weight has lifted with the knowledge that Elena is safe in my bed and that the rapist got what was coming to him. Though I'd be more satisfied if he wasn't breathing. I dry my hands and go downstairs.

I join the men at the table. Demon has a radiant smile on his face. I try to smother a smile at the fact that violence makes him a happy boy.

"Care to explain what the fuck happened?" Reaper asks.

I'm honest. The men need to know. "We got to Elena's just in time before her boss raped her."

There're gasps, then silence around the table. Demon's still smiling, but the rest of the men's faces harden. No one dares to argue the point. Everyone would have done the same if that happened to their girl.

Reaper nods. "That explains it, then. Our contact at the police station called and informed me that a man got stabbed, and two men wearing cuts were seen leaving the scene."

Demon snorts. "They're exaggerating. I only stabbed his hands for touching Elena."

"Nice job," Viper chimes in.

"Thanks," Demon replies, looking pleased with himself. "I would have done more, but there were too many witnesses. I can go back now if you want me to?"

"I'm down for that," I swiftly respond.

"Not now. Will her boss report the two of you to the police?" Bomber asks, glancing at me and then Demon.

"I doubt it," Demon replies. "I warned him if he talks, I'll chop off his fingers one by one and shove them down his throat."

"Jesus Christ," Twitch mutters.

I laugh because I truly believe Demon would do it.

"Is there anything else anyone would like to add?" asks Reaper.

I shake my head. No one says anything, so Reaper bangs the gavel and we all get up to leave.

Cash puts his hand on my arm. "How is she?"

"He would have raped her if we hadn't shown up," I say through gritted teeth, anger flaring. I stretch my neck from side to side, trying to calm myself as the rapid mood change threatens to drown me. "It's shaken her up."

He shakes his head, disgust written all over his face. "Did he get far?"

"I haven't asked. Elena had her clothes on. She was terrified, her hair was a mess around her head, and her shirt was pulled up, showing her bra. She was so drunk"—I swallow thickly—"she wouldn't have been able to put up much of a fight."

He frowns. "I'm glad you got there when you did."

"Me too." But if I hadn't made the bet, I guarantee she wouldn't have been drinking. Elena hardly drinks. This is my fault. "I better get back and check on her," I say.

I rush to Elena, taking the stairs two at a time. I open the bedroom door slowly, not wanting to wake her. The room is dark, but with the light filtering in the window, it's still bright enough to see her.

I take off my cut, then my shirt, and get under the blanket with her. She rolls over toward me and shuffles close. I put my arm around her, pulling her tight against me. I'll do anything to make it right. "I love you, Elena," I whisper. "I promise to make it up to you."

I wake up to sunlight flooding the room and Elena moving in my arms. She stiffens. I lie on my side so that we're facing each other and rub her back, giving her a minute. But then I hear sniffling. I cup her chin and raise her head. Tears streak her face. Her grief pierces my heart. "Do you remember?" I ask.

"Yes," she whispers.

I lean in and kiss her forehead. "You're safe now."

"You came for me . . ." Her voice cracks. "Thank you."

"I'll always protect you." Hell, I'd kill for her . . . I wanted to kill for her. I remember the blood pouring from his face as I lay into him with my fists. That will have to do . . . *for now.*

"Are you hungry?" I ask. "Do you want some food or water . . . or maybe a headache pill?" Lately, I've become very familiar with what a hangover feels like.

"No. I just want you here with me."

"Of course I'll stay with you, baby girl."

She grasps my hand and links our fingers together. She's

staring at my bruised knuckles and the cuts on my hand. "I'm sorry you got hurt."

I briefly close my eyes. "It was worth it." I feel a sense of regret, like I didn't do enough. Her boss should be dead, but at the same time I didn't want to bring too much heat on the club, and Elena needed me.

"What did Demon do to him?" she asks.

"Uh . . . you sure you want to know?" I give her an out because she's not used to violence.

"Yes," she replies firmly.

"Demon stabbed him in the hands for laying a hand on you."

She's quiet, making me think I shouldn't have told her.

"I can't go back to work . . ." she mumbles.

"You certainly won't be." *No fucking way!*

She stares down before making eye contact. "What happened to Cameron?" She shudders. "I'm going to find it hard if I run into him again."

My jaw clenches. I swear if I see that guy again, I'll strangle him. "He's gone and won't be coming back."

She frowns. "What makes you so sure?"

"Because Demon made it pretty clear that we wanted to kill him and that we will if he ever comes back to this town. Hell, I hope he comes back."

Tears fall from her eyes. It kills me seeing her like this.

"Do you think Lucy and all of them knew . . . knew of Cameron's past, but still let him walk me to my room drunk?"

"I have no idea, but I'm sure your boss would have denied everything to anyone who ever asked about his past."

She nods slowly. "I don't want to live with my roommates anymore, in the house where it happened, either."

"You don't have to. I told you to move in here." I don't want to sound like I'm pressuring her, so I add, "At least until you get back on your feet so that you don't have to pay rent." But really, I want her to stay with me forever.

"Thank you so much," she whispers. Hurt still lingers in her voice.

All I want to do is take her pain away. "Whatever you need. Just say when, and me and one of the men will go pack up your things and bring them to the clubhouse."

"Soon please. I just . . . I just want that all behind me. Cameron's friends with my roommates, and I don't want to associate with any of them."

"Me and Cash will go tomorrow."

She squeezes my hand. "Okay, I need you here holding me today, though."

"I'm not going anywhere." If she wants me, I'll never leave her side again.

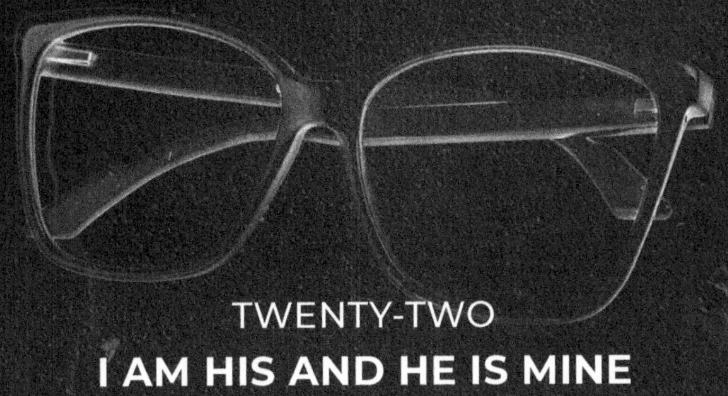

TWENTY-TWO
I AM HIS AND HE IS MINE

Elena

A MONTH PASSES BY, AND WITH EACH DAY I FEEL STRONGER. MY anxiety got worse after the incident, to the point where I was curled up in bed with Axle by my side. His presence calmed me. His unwavering support has been my anchor through it all, and I've slowly pieced myself back together.

I've seen the sincerity of his regret, so I forgave him and chose to move on from our past mistakes, this time without any lies or bets. He hurt me, but he's given me my confidence back, and the whole time I've been with him he's protected me and shown me how much he loves me.

The clubhouse is now my home. The men here are my friends . . . well, most of them. I'm still a little unsure about Bomber and Demon. Grace and Vera have been quieter than usual. I still get the daggers from Grace, and I'm sure it's only a matter of time before she starts being nasty again. I'm not going to let it get to me, and I know I need to work on sticking up for myself.

I'm on Axle's lap outside. We're sitting at the table and he's laughing and talking to the men. I smile at my red flag of a soul mate. The more I'm with him, the more I feel like myself. It's as if I was comatose and he breathed air into my soul. I've changed since I met him, but in a good way. Our love doesn't make sense, but I love who I am when I'm with him, and that's all that matters.

He gives me an adoring smile, then plants a hard kiss on my lips and hugs me tightly. "I fucking love you. You know that, right?"

"Yes," I reply. I smile. He tells me every day.

"We should get married."

I cough. His words have gotten stuck in my throat. "Did you just propose to me?" I ask in utter shock. There's silence around the table.

He smiles wickedly. "Yeah, why not?"

"You don't mean it," I playfully whack him. "You're just joking."

He shakes his head. His playfulness is gone. "You're my ride or die, babe, and you make me a better person. Just being around you calms my restless soul. I know Victor would kick my ass if I let you slip through my fingers."

"Say yes, darl'. You know you want to," Viper chimes in.

"Oh, what the hell—yes!" I beam and his entire face brightens. His lips meet mine. He kisses me longer this time, but with a gentle tenderness. He's got a smart mouth and he's a little crazy, but I can't imagine my life without him. He showed me how to live. I showed him how to love.

IN TRUE AXLE FASHION, WITH HIS RECKLESSNESS AND impulsivity, he demanded we get married within a week. I've managed to organize a wedding in a hall in town. I went with minimal decorations, and a couple of the club members helped to set it up. I purchased my wedding dress online with express delivery. I thought I'd want a big wedding with all the bells and whistles, but I realized that all I want is my friends—who have turned into family—and my sister there. All the rest doesn't matter.

"It's going to be okay tomorrow, babe. Stop stressing," Axle says beside me on the bed.

I scoff. *Easy for him to say.* "I hope my parents don't ruin it for us." The phone call with them was an absolute nightmare. My mom, as per usual, was overly dramatic and had to be taken to the hospital by ambulance. My sister called me to say it was just a panic attack.

"Are they even going to come?" he asks.

"Ava said they would, but as you know, I don't want Dad walking me down the aisle. It doesn't seem right if they don't support us as a couple."

Axle's eyes narrow. "As if I'd let them ruin our wedding. I've talked to the men about keeping an eye on them. You've got nothing to worry about."

I breathe a sigh of relief. He's always protecting me. Thinking of my sister warms my chest. "I'm so excited to see my sister."

"Babe," he says mockingly, "you're supposed to be excited to marry me. Anyone would think you're more excited to see her."

I laugh, then wrap my arms around his shoulders and plant a kiss on his lips. "Of course I'm excited to marry you. It's just that I haven't seen or spoken to her properly in a really long time. She got married and eventually we stopped talking." I miss spending time with her so much.

"Fuck her," he says with a bite in his tone. "You deserve better than that."

"Axle," I warn. "She's a kind, loving person. You'll see! I reckon it's her husband that's created the distance between us. When I see them, there's something off about him. I just don't trust him."

Axle nods. "Always trust your instincts."

My eyes narrow. "And talking about my sister . . ."

He inches back. "Woah, why are you giving me that look?"

"Ava is beautiful. I want none of the MC men trying to hit on her. I know she's married, but I'm sure that wouldn't stop them."

"I can't promise—"

My eyes narrow further into slits.

He chuckles. "Okay, okay. I'll warn them beforehand."

"Promise me?" I don't need drama. My sister would never cheat, but she's a kind person, and I don't want any of the men trying anything. Her husband is overprotective of her, and I don't want any fights.

Axle puts a cross over his heart. "I promise."

I look away, thinking. "I know it's short notice, but I'd still like someone to walk me down the aisle. Do you think if I ask Cash he'll say yes?"

Axle's eyes bulge. "You sure?"

I nod. "It seems right. The whole time, Cash has encouraged us to be together, and he's your best friend. He's always been friendly and welcoming to me, and I'd like it to be someone who believes in us as a couple and who cares about us." It is my wedding . . . my time to be happy.

"Cash would be honored." Axle leans over and kisses my cheek. "Thank you for thinking about me too." There's a tenderness in his words, and I know he means it.

He stands and grabs my hand, pulling me to my feet. "Let's go downstairs and have a few drinks to celebrate with the men. Tomorrow you will be Mrs. Elena Evans."

I smile widely at him. I can't wait for tomorrow. When we reach the top of the stairs, I see all the MC men are around the bar. When their eyes catch us, they cheer and clap. Viper's hollering. Heat rises up my neck and to my cheeks, but I'm smiling. As I step down the stairs, I trip on the first one. My stomach plummets, but two hands come around my waist and pull me upright.

"I've got you, babe," Axle says with a wink. He yells out to the crowd, "She's always falling for me."

The men and I start laughing. I swat at the cheeky devil. We've been on a wild ride. After all the love and deceit, the joy and heartbreak, I still love him. I'm happiest and most confident when I'm with him.

TWENTY-THREE
COMMITMENT

Elena

TODAY IS THE BIG DAY. I'M AN ABSOLUTE MESS. I HAVEN'T SEEN Axle. I need his reassurance right now. Cash and I are outside, waiting for the music to play, to go inside.

"Is there anything I can do to . . . um . . . help you?" Cash asks, his eyes wide. He's keeping his distance from me.

I shake my head. My skin is on fire. I flap my arms, trying to cool down my armpits because I'm sweating up a storm. I hope I don't leave marks on my satin wedding dress. I went with an elegant, white, off-the-shoulder mermaid dress with a short train.

"Do you want me to cancel the wedding?" he asks.

"No!" I reply. My voice is harsh. "I want to get married to Axle. I'm just anxious about walking down the aisle while everyone's looking at me. I'm not good with being the center of attention." I close my eyes. "And what if Axle changes his mind?" I suck in a sharp breath, my heart threatening to burst. "What if he realizes he doesn't want to spend the rest of his life with me? What if—"

"He loves you," Cash says soothingly, his hands on my shoulders. "Everything is going to be o-kay."

I take deep breaths, but my mind tortures me. "What happened to my parents? Are they here? Is my sister here?" I hope my sister's here. I don't want to do today without her.

"Yes, Viper said they're sitting in the front row. Rage is by their side, keeping an eye on your parents so that they behave. Everything is under control."

"Wicked Game" by Chris Isaak begins to play. It's the instrumental version. I thought it was appropriate given our love story. Cash holds his arm out and I link mine with his, then pull him close to me. "Don't let me fall . . ." Because it is highly likely I'll trip over my own feet, especially in these heels.

He chuckles. "I won't let you fall."

I peer up at him to see his soft, reassuring gaze. I smile, grateful I chose him to walk me down the aisle.

One slow step at a time we make our way in and down. I keep my eyes on the incredible man at the end of it. I know everyone is looking at me, so I put all my focus on Axle. He's facing me. He's wearing normal attire—dark jeans, a white shirt with his cut over the top—and I'm fine with that. I don't want to force him to change. I want him to be himself. It's his day too.

I glance at the front row. My sister is smiling widely and dabbing the corner of her eye like she's crying. When we reach Axle, Cash hands me off to him. Axle gazes at me adoringly. My anxiety floats away in his presence and at seeing his love for me. I know deep in my soul that I made the right decision to marry him, and I've never been so certain of something in my life.

Axle slowly raises his hand to my cheek, and I nuzzle into it. "You look beautiful, baby girl."

I blink back tears. We aren't even married yet and I'm barely holding back my emotions. *Don't cry, don't cry.*

His eyes devour every inch of me. He arches his neck and peers around the side to see my ass. "And that dress . . ." He whistles and wipes the sweat off his forehead, giving me his signature grin. He pulls me into him, then his eyes flick to my lips, and before I can utter a single word, his lips are on mine in a slow, tender kiss.

The priest clears his voice, and then I hear, "You're not supposed to kiss her yet." I instantly know the voice from the crowd belongs to Viper.

I pull back, giggling. It's so typical of Axle.

"You taste delicious," he says wickedly. "Are you ready to be Mrs. Evans?"

"I'm so ready to spend the rest of my life with you."

Axle

I PEER AROUND THE CROWD. THE RECEPTION SEEMS TO BE GOING well. I sigh while I look at *my* wife. Fuck, I'm lucky she gave me a second chance and said yes when I asked her to marry me. She's talking to her sister, Ava, at our table. They both laugh, then take a sip of their champagne. I smile at them. Elena looks so happy with Ava.

I thought I was going to hate Ava for how she's treated Elena, but she's sweet and quiet, just like Elena. The two of them have stayed close all night. I look over at Ava's husband. He's a drunk. I have no idea how he managed to score someone like her. The only reason we haven't kicked his ass out is because I don't want to upset Ava, which will then upset Elena, but I've had the men keep a close eye on him.

Viper and Reaper have taken a liking to Ava. I was in shock when Reaper sounded interested. He's never shown interest in any woman since I've met him. I'm just praying to God they listen to me and leave Ava alone. Tonight is my wife's night, and I have to ensure she has the perfect night with no drama.

Elena's parents haven't caused any issues, but even if they tried, we have them under control. They haven't spoken a word to me, which I find hilarious. They haven't hugged Elena or congratulated her, not that I'm surprised. They've just been stone-cold quiet. I think they came just to show their faces, but I'm betting we won't be seeing much of them in the future.

The music suddenly changes to a dirty dancing beat. Reaper is on the microphone. "Everyone, it's time for tossing the bouquet and the garter."

I rub my hands together. My body tingles with anticipation. "The garter first," I yell out. There's a round of chuckles. When Elena looks at me, she smiles. I wink back and give her an indecent grin.

She stands while I move to her. We link hands, and I lean down to give her a brief kiss. As we walk toward the chair in the middle of the dance floor, I say. "Can we get out of here soon? I want you all to myself."

She gives me a knowing smile. "You'll be alright. There's only a few more hours to go."

I snort. "No, I won't be, and this is just going to be a tease."

When we reach the chair, Elena sits. The crowd hums with excitement.

"Over here," Cash calls out. He's holding a blindfold.

"What's that for?" I ask.

"It's to go over your eyes."

I frown. "I don't need that."

"It's a request from your wife."

Well . . . in that case, I don't have a choice. *"Fine!"*

He places the blindfold over my head, covering my eyes. My anticipation heightens.

"Can you see?" he asks.

"Nope!"

"Good," he chuckles.

There's a pause and I'm buzzin'. "Well, can I go to my wife yet or what?"

"Just hold on a sec."

I groan. "What do I have to wait for?" They are teasing me on purpose, I swear. I tap my foot.

"Okay . . . it's time. I'll grab your arm and lead you to her."

My heartbeat quickens. I lick my lips in eagerness. I can't wait to touch her soft, smooth legs.

"Here's Elena," Cash says.

I kneel down, lift her dress, and grab her foot. The crowd cheers. I breathe in . . . Jesus Christ . . . I near gag at the stench. I keep going further, past her calf muscle. I want this to be sexy, so I start to run my tongue up her leg to the garter. Wait . . . her legs are hairy AF! How did the hair grow so fast? She wasn't like that the other day. But I keep going, and when I reach her thigh, I tug the soft material down her leg with my teeth. When I get up, the crowd is in stitches laughing.

I slip off the blindfold to find—to my horror—Viper sitting on the chair with a tablecloth on his lap. He blows me a kiss. I shake my head as my stomach churns. Elena is laughing. She and Viper high-five each other. I turn to the side, gagging again.

Viper gets off the chair and steps over to me. "You loved it, brother."

"You've scarred me for life. I'm going to have nightmares."

Elena comes over, wearing a smug grin.

I raise my brow. "That wasn't very nice, Mrs. Evans."

She laughs. "Oh, *babe*, that was hysterical."

No doubt it's payback for all the times I embarrassed her. At least she's got a sense of humor. I suppose she'd have to to put up with all my shit.

The end.

Did you want to go into the draw to win a *free paperback*? Sign up for my mailing list. Simply opening my newsletter emails enters you to win any paperback.

If you love my books, please leave a *review* or *rating* on your purchased retailer or your favorite platform. It encourages other readers to take a chance on me. It truly makes a difference and provides crucial feedback.

SNEAK PEEK AT REAPER

Reaper

I want her.

Those curves. That smile. I've never been so attracted to a woman. I take a swig of my beer and watch as she talks to her sister, Elena. We are at Elena and Axle's wedding. The men mentioned Elena had a sister, but I have never seen her before today, and I know I won't be forgetting her anytime soon. She leans in, picks up her champagne, and takes a few sips. When she places it on the table, the strap of her dress falls from her shoulder, and all I want to do is taste her.

I readjust myself in my seat.

Viper elbows me. "You like her?" He gives Elena's sister a pointed look.

Bomber leans in from the other side of me, listening to our conversation.

"I do." I want her badly.

"Her name's Ava," says Viper.

I raise a brow, and he grins smugly.

"What?" he says with his hands up. "She's fucking hot, so of course I asked Axle about her."

My jaw clenches. The possessiveness shooting through me surprises me. I don't even know her. I glance at Bomber, and the side of his lip twitches like he's smothering a smirk. The observant bastard misses nothing.

"She's married," Viper chimes in. "Not that it means anything these days."

I lift my hand to my chin. "I wonder how committed."

"Axle didn't say, but he warned me to stay away. He said—and I quote—'I want to have sex with my wife tonight, and I don't want anyone fucking that up for me. So Ava's off limits.'" Viper's voice mocks Axle's.

Ava is still deep in conversation with Elena; then they laugh. The music is too loud, so I can't hear them, but it makes me curious as to what her laugh sounds like.

"Is her husband here?" I ask Viper.

He laughs. "It's the guy sitting next to Elena's mom at the table next to the bride and groom."

I peer at Elena's parents and see a man gulping half of his bottle of beer next to them. His eyes are on Ava.

"She's with the drunk?" I ask, shocked, remembering the man stumbling to the bar earlier.

"Yep. I couldn't believe it either. She's way too good for him."

I stare at the man who has what I want. He's average looking, nothing special.

"I saw him earlier, but I thought he was a family member."

I haven't seen him touch or kiss Ava or show any affection that would suggest they're married. If she was mine, I wouldn't be able to keep my hands off her. I'd want the world to know.

"Viper," Candy calls from the dance floor. "Come and dance with me."

His smile widens. "I'm coming." He stands. "Well, fellas, it's my time to shine."

Chuckling, I shake my head.

He fixes his hair like he's a peacock parading its feathers. "What? I've got moves."

"Yeah, okay, Justin Timberlake," I taunt.

He walks to Candy, puts his arm across her back, and dips her backward, lifting a brow and grinning at us. She lets out a squeal and laughs.

Demon's leaning back in his chair, looking at the dance floor. He doesn't look like he's watching people dancing; it's like he sees through them, as if his mind is elsewhere. He taps on the table, and even with his tattoos, bruises and scabs on his knuckles from the other night stand out.

I lean toward him and raise my voice. "You don't have to stay here."

He slowly turns his head with a wicked smile and then stands. He lifts his chin. "I'll see you back at the clubhouse later."

With a sharp nod, I watch as people step away from him, giving him room to move freely to the exit.

I make eye contact with Axle. He leaves a group and walks to us.

"Is Demon leaving already?" He looks at his watch. "It's still early."

"He looked bored, which is usually not good."

He sighs. "Good point."

"Is Ava really married?" I ask, hoping Viper got it wrong.

Axle's eyes widen. "You too?" His shoulders drop. "Just give me one night of wild sex with my wife. I don't want her in my ear saying that her sister had sex with a biker and got divorced over it." His voice is whiney.

Even though it's tempting, I respect Axle too much to do anything about it, but something claws inside of me. "You have my word."

He blows out a gush of air. Elena appears at his side. He looks at her, smiles, and puts his arm around her waist. "You owe me a dance."

She smiles back. "I thought you'd never ask."

He grabs her hand and leads her to the dance floor.

I search for Ava but can't find her. I sit upright in my chair, looking around. "She walked toward the restroom," says Bomber, like he read my mind. We've been friends for a long time. We know each other well.

"Thanks," I reply, my eyes turning to the hallway leading to the bathroom. I fidget in my chair, wanting to get up, but the discussion I had with Axle keeps me seated.

I may never see her again plays in my head. I've never felt a strong pull to a woman before, so I stop fighting myself and then stride toward the restrooms. I won't have sex with her anyway. I'm just curious.

As I get closer, she walks out. Her eyes are on her dress as she tries to pull up its cleavage. Her dress covers most of her boobs, but with big perfect tits like that, I don't know why she is bothering. She looks flawless the way it is.

She huffs when the dress won't cover her further. When she lifts her eyes, they widen when she sees me staring at her, and it's like someone has punched me in the gut.

"You're beautiful."

Freezing, Ava stares at me with wide eyes. She says nothing, but a blush creeps up her neck and to her face. She breaks eye contact as she picks at her dress. When she looks up at me, she smiles and her eyes glisten like she's holding back tears. "Thank you."

In my periphery, her husband approaches us with narrowed eyes, though swaying to the right. The warmth in my chest dissipates, and my body tenses and turns to stone. I glance at Ava, and when her eyes lock onto her husband, she gasps and steps away from me. Her breathing has picked up. Her shoulders have hunched over, and she looks scared.

I fucking hate it. Something isn't right.

When he reaches us, I can smell the alcohol on him. He looks me up and down with his glassy eyes, and I don't miss the tightness in his jaw.

His hand comes out to me. "Beau."

I shake his hand, noticing his firm grip. "Reaper."

He coughs. "Well, that's certainly a name you've got there."

I ignore him and look at Ava. She swallows thickly as her eyes keep darting between me and her husband.

"I'm ready to go, Ava. Your parents are leaving, too."

My eyes widen. No "are you ready to leave?" It seems like an order.

"You can stay with your sister. There are spare rooms available," I tell her.

He answers for her. "Ava's tired." Then he looks at her. "Aren't you?"

"Ah, yes," she replies and gives me a small smile. "But I appreciate the offer."

Beau grabs her arm. She flinches. My hands clench at my side.

"Have a good night," she says before they turn and leave.

It takes everything in me to stay still, to not rip her away from him. My gut churns.

Something isn't right; she fears him.

I close my eyes briefly. "She's not mine," I say to myself. "She's not mine."

Grab your copy of Reaper now.

RESOURCES

One Australian dollar of every paperback book purchase from Bianca's website will go to the LifeLine charity.

If you are struggling with your mental health, contact Life-Line. LifeLine is available in many countries and offers help for people experiencing emotional distress. They provide confidential crisis support, and in most instances, you can call, chat online, or text.

Please visit https://lifeline-intl.com/our-network/ for more information.

If you are seeking help with a drinking problem, contact Alcoholics Anonymous. AA is an informal society that operates in many countries and offers peer support for recovery from alcoholism.

Please visit https://www.aa.org/find-aa/world for more information.

ACKNOWLEDGMENTS

To my family, thank you for putting up with my mood swings and anxiety during the writing process 😊

To the readers, I hope you loved Elena and Axle's story. I enjoyed writing it. Thank you for your support and patience waiting for my new releases. The manuscript undergoes review by three editors and beta readers to ensure high quality before publication, making it a lengthy process.

Thank you, Silvia and the beta readers for feedback and Jana at Proofreading Services for my book editing, as well as Maria for my covers and interior graphics. They are all dedicated and do such a great job.

Kind regards,

Bianca Lee Ward

ABOUT THE AUTHOR

Bianca Lee Ward is an Australian romance author with a love of culinary adventures and a playlist for every mood. She enjoys exploring themes of identity, personal growth, and resilience in her work—with a little spice on the side. When she isn't lost in storytelling or absorbed in her latest read, Bianca can be found watching true crime stories and documentaries.

You can connect with Bianca online at:
Website: www.biancaleeward.com
Email: info@biancaleeward.com
Instagram: https://www.instagram.com/biancaleeward
Facebook: https://www.facebook.com/biancaleeward
Spotify: Bianca Lee Ward
Pinterest: https://www.pinterest.com.au/biancaleeward
Goodreads: https://www.goodreads.com/author/show/30477361.Bianca_Lee_Ward
BookBub: https://www.bookbub.com/authors/bianca-lee-ward

Don't forget to sign up to Bianca's mailing list, where you'll get *huge* discounts, *exclusive* giveaways, and new release alerts!